Francis Turner Palgrave

Amenophis and other Poems

sacred and secular

Francis Turner Palgrave

Amenophis and other Poems
sacred and secular

ISBN/EAN: 9783337397968

Printed in Europe, USA, Canada, Australia, Japan

Cover: Foto ©Andreas Hilbeck / pixelio.de

More available books at **www.hansebooks.com**

AMENOPHIS

AND

OTHER POEMS

CRED AND SECULAR

BY

FRANCIS T. PALGRAVE

PROFESSOR OF POETRY IN THE UNIVERSITY OF OXFORD

London

MACMILLAN AND CO.

AND NEW YORK

1892

CONTENTS

HYMNS

AND

MEDITATIONS

—To write true, unfeignéd verse,
Is very hard—
HENRY VAUGHAN : *Silex Scintillans*

B

Some of the following pieces are printed, (with revision), from the series published in 1870 : Others have appeared dispersedly.

Aug. 1892

Little Park, Lyme Regis

Dorset

ON LYME BEACH

URANIA, voice of Heaven within the heart!
    Urania fair, that art
Silent amid thy sisters, yet alone
To man then audible
When the sad ear rejects all earthly tone ;—

When the last farewell sigh of wife or child
Leaves us unreconciled ;
When the gray death-mists o'er our own weak eyes
Fold, and the Star of Faith
Burns o'er the gulph that sheer before us lies :—

O shrined by Hellas in her central shrine,
By Milton named divine,
By us, yet, meaner men, thy voice is heard
At times, as the faint cry
Dropp'd dewlike from the twilight-wheeling bird :—

B 2

Mid life's low dust and din we hear that cry,
And start to find thee nigh ;
As in some rock-hewn den the sunlit blue
Through rifts peers in, and tells
Of higher worlds than this, and life more true.

—Sweet summer moon, that pours on this fair bay
A fairer light than day,
O'er yon still sea thy steady gleam in flakes
Of orange-silver laid
Down one long path just heaves, and heaving breaks,

And, broken, reunites itself:—and then
I hear again, again,
The great tenth wave with one long impulse smite
Whole miles of bay, and send
The voice of central ocean through the night.

Remote at once and near, the muffled roar
Intones around the shore :
Then the wing'd tribes that call the night their day
With elfin pipings pass ;
And then again the billow smites the bay.

As when the seven bold chiefs Prydéri led,[1]
Bearing Brân's sacred head,
At Harlech in Ardudwy, music-bound,
Sat year on year, and heard
Rhiannon's feather'd quire : O'erseas the sound

1 See Note

Murmur'd, far-floating ; yet in each man's ear
Rang sweet and close and clear ;
And they forgot their slaughter'd comrades brave
On Erin's fatal field,
And the white-bosom'd Bronwen's long-hid grave,

Listening :—E'en so o'er us, in this fair bay,
Their spell the sea-sounds lay,
Recalling how the fresh Ionian breeze
To that great sightless seer[1]
Who sang the shadowy hills and sounding seas,

Bore the same voice, and spoke of other powers
And other worlds than ours ;
As if some oracle in that rhythmic wave
Told how, through all the noise
Of those who cry, and boast, and laugh, and rave,

The Eternal Order makes His music clear
To hearts that choose to hear ;
And though in His high pleasure He withdraw
Himself behind Himself,
Yet through all worlds is love, and life, and law.

—Eugenia ! Singly dearest ! Not as, while
In love's first hour, a smile
Of glory brighten'd earth, we see it now :
The dream is gone : and we
Calmly the bitter, better truth avow.

E'en yet. life's journey to the children dear
Looks summer-mid-day clear :
But taught by stumbling steps, we know the way
Has no more light at best
Than these low moonbeams on the billows gray,

The dusking hills, and skies that darker grow
As the stars keenlier glow :—
Only within the heart Urania's voice
Wakens a chord at times,
And thy hand meets in mine, and we rejoice

Sedately : and we know the faith we hold
Was, before Time, enroll'd
In God's own archives : and the dawn's soft breeze
Smites cool upon the brow,
And Heaven's first day-smile trembles o'er the seas.

QUATUOR NOVISSIMA

Argument

Death ; Judgment ; Heaven ; Hell :—Man would despair of
life if he really realized these, as was attempted by some
of old.—The tradition of Glamis Castle.—The Chartreuse
of Saint Bruno near Grenoble.—Such a life now scantly
possible, nor, for mankind generally, in the truest accordance with Nature. Our detachment from the world must
be while in the world.—Earthly and heavenly comforts as
aids to life and death in Christ.

B EFORE these human eyes
    Could that dread Vision rise,
Those four last Terrors all mankind must know ;
    The ghastly grave : The Throne
    And He Who is thereon :
The verdict-voice of God, dividing weal from woe :

    Scarce could we turn or care
    To look upon this fair
And varied earth,—this laughing sea and sky ;
    On Nature's genial face
    The Fate-mark we should trace,—
A rose-crown'd victim led unconscious forth to die !

That long, long, trumpet-thrill
Our trembling ears must fill,
Gainst voice of man and joy of music steel'd :—
Life's motley moving show
Too poor would seem, too low
For eyes to that vast world beyond the world unseal'd.

As who in manhood's hour
Within the fateful tower
Goes, not returning what he went :   For he
On that has dared to gaze
Which twilights all his days,
And turns the whole vain world to vainer vanity :

So on our mortal sight
If Thou should'st choose to smite
The fearful things to come, too clear, too nigh,
The heaven-dishearten'd soul
Would faint to near the goal ;
Before Death's Gorgon face sweet life to stone would
die.

O 'tis in mercy, then,
Thou hast withheld from men
The sacred terrors of the final day :
The weight of too much truth
Would crush the flowers of youth,
And blight the fruits of age, the crown of life's decay !

So keep the mercy-veil,
Lest our sad spirits fail,
Dead ere our day before the dread To-be :—
Let Thy soft gracious cloud
The black horizon shroud,
Thy bow o'erarch the vale, and bid us rest in Thee !

—Yet those we blame not, they
Who in earth's earlier day
And nearer Christ,—fleeing to wold and waste,
With the whole heart's whole power
Fore-lived their life's last hour,
Thirsting before the time the gulphs of death to taste.

I see the climbing road
Which from Isère he trode,
Bruno, while on the heights a home he seeks :
Rock-sown the vale and rude,
The soul of solitude ;
Gray shiver'd walls around, and Angel-haunted peaks

There in the twilight low
The white-robed brothers go,
And meet and pass,—no sign, no look, no word :
Only they lift their sight
Tow'rd the loved cross-crown'd height,
And pierce beyond the blue, and see the ascended
    Lord.

There in dim granite cave,
To Fancy's eye the grave
Of some forgotten far-off warrior wild,
Circling the saintly head
The light of Heaven is shed,
As in the Mother's arms he sees the Eternal Child.

And though the final Fear
Gloom near and yet more near
As days from life's fast-falling rosary slip ;
Yet in that Faith and Friend
Secure, he sights the end,—
God's pardon and award from his Redeemer's lip.

—Not in the wild, not so
Our later footsteps go,
Doom'd to the garish world, the vulgar sphere !
The dull worn ways, the strife
And highway-dust of life,
Such is thy lot, O Man !—thine heritage is here !

For not this globe alone
Pursues a track unknown,
Whirl'd by our Monarch Star through bound-
less space :
Man's heart is drawn by God
In lines of old untrod ;
Fresh paths to Heaven disclosed before the changing
race.

—Where man cannot intrude
We have our solitude ;
The heart of heart, the inviolate inner shrine :
We call on Thee, and there
The soul Thou canst prepare
To face the Four Last Things, veil'd o'er by Love
divine :

From sight veil'd o'er, that so
With steadier fuller flow
Life's river to the eternal sea may stream :—
Uncheck'd by terror chill,
That we the field may till,
A man's work while 'tis day, ere night unyoke the
team.

A man's full year-long task,—
Not less than this we ask,
Lest sloth enrust the soul, unstirr'd and still :
Unknown, or known ; low ; high ;
Beneath the Master's eye
'Tis one, if wrought for Him, with joy of earnest will.

Lift from our hearts the gloom
Of that near-yawning tomb !
The song of birds, the flower at our feet,
All precious things and fair
We need, life's weight to bear ;
The heaven-lit light of home, the smiles of children
sweet.

And in Thy holy place
Thou dost unfold the grace
Strong in that hour to comfort and to save :
We see the Victim die,
The Lord gone up on high,
The life-in-death of Christ,--the glory of the grave !

—Then keep the mercy-veil,
Lest our faint spirits fail,
Dead ere our day before the dread To-be :—
Till the soft hand of Love
The shroud of earth remove,
All tears wiped from all eyes ;—the Soul at rest with
Thee.

III

AT EPHESUS

. . . Vidi un veglio solo
Venir dormendo con la faccia arguta.

OF those that saw Him, when
On common earth He trod
The life of man with men,
I only, only, breathe,
Who lean'd upon His breast, and knew that He was
God.

As some strange thing that lies
Surviving all his kind,
I, 'neath the radiant skies,
Crawl baby-weak once more,
Stranded upon my hundred years of life, and blind.

And as that beast could tell
Of old incredible shapes
That peopled lake and dell;
Seas, where rocks climb the sky,
And azure ice-hills where the parch'd Sahara gapes :

So John can testify,
Alone of living men,
By seeing of the eye
And hearing of the ear,
That very God as man breathed, died, and rose again.

It was the time foreshown ;
Like a new sun o'er earth,—
Beyond all wonders known
Wonder most wonderful,—
The Well-Belovéd came, the Babe of heavenly birth.

He did the deeds, He spoke
The words past human wit :
Then gently slipp'd the yoke
Of flesh, and went to God ;
And we our treasure found, only when losing it.

Yet, though the Word withdrew,
The Paraclete remain'd ;
Christ's nearness oft we knew ;
Enough to guide our life
From thought of how He spoke, and how He loved,
  we gain'd.

And once, 'tis said, o'er one
As though born out of time
The glory-vision shone,
Journeying Damascus-way ;
Who lived in Christ, and died in some far westward
  clime.

Of breathing witnesses
Survives now none but I ;
Who heard the Master bless
The bread and wine of life ;
Saw Him and touch'd, betwixt the sepulchre and the
sky.

—But though the faith of Sight
By natural law must fail,
A heavenlier higher light
Upon the soul will dawn ;
The unseen outshine the seen ; the faith of Fai
prevail.

The things of sense are much ;
But more the things of mind :
What we but see or touch
Less real, durable, true,
Than that invisible all-sustaining Life behind :

As one of Athens taught
In his own ethnic way,
That all things here were nought
But shadowy images
Of forms that in the eternal Wisdom living lay.

When these dim eyes are closed,
Children ! Remember well
The word that John imposed
With his last lips on you,
To walk henceforth by faith, and grasp the invisible.

What if no more the Lord
Before the last dread day
Be seen, yet shall His word
Its might and music keep ;
Shall find fit echo in the heart of heart for aye.

As, in due transit, by
The milestone-years ye go,
Though star-like fix'd on high
The cross and He thereon
Down Time's gray avenue further, fainter, show :—

If then the Lord delays,
O yet ye need not fear,
Faint hearts of latter days !
Time cannot touch the love
To which a thousand years but one brief hour appear.

As age on age unrolls,
If faith her light withdraw
From present-bounded souls
Who only dare believe
What they themselves have seen, or hold for Nature's
    law ;

Or those who will not raise,
E'en as they cry for light,
Their heads o'er life's hot haze,
Nor care to see the stars,
Mute witnesses for God, nor dawning after night :—

Yet oft in that dark hour
When first the unseen is felt,
The Word will come in power,
The so-far-off draw nigh,
Christ's living love the long doubt-frozen bosom melt.

—O living Love, so near
On earth, so near above,
In Thy good time appear,
Take all Thy children home,—
Who love, yet know Thee not ;—who, faithful, bow,
and love !

—My little children true !
Before these lips are dumb
They leave this word for you,
Love one another ! And
Again, Love one another ! . . . Enough ; He calls : I
come.

IV

THE REIGN OF LAW

THE dawn goes up the sky
  Like any other day ;
And these have only come
  To mourn Him where He lay.
—" We ne'er have seen the law
  Reversed, 'neath which we lie ;
Exceptions none are found,
  And when we die, we die.
Resign'd to fact we wander hither ;
We ask no more the whence and whither.

" Vain questions ! from the first
  Put, and no answer found.
He binds us with the chain
  Wherewith Himself is bound.
From west to east the earth
  Unrolls her primal curve
The sun himself were vex'd
  Did she one furlong swerve :
The myriad years have whirl'd her hither,
But tell not of the whence and whither.

" We know but what we see,
  Like cause, and like event ;

One constant force runs on
   Transmuted, but unspent :
From her own laws the mind
   Infers a conscious plan ;
Deducing from within
   God's special thought for man :
The natural choice that brought us hither
Is silent on the whence and whither.

  " If God there be, or Gods,
    Without our science lies :
We cannot see or touch,
   Measure, nor analyse.
Life is but what we live ;
   We know but what we know :
Souls prison'd each in self
   Whether God be, or no :
The self-moved force that bore us hither
Reveals no whence, and hints no whither.

  " Ah, which is likelier truth,
    That law should hold its way,
Or, for this One of all,
   Life reassert her sway ?
Like any other morn
   The sun goes up the sky ;
No crisis marks the day ;
   For when we die, we die.
No fair fond hope allures us hither ;
The law is dumb on whence and whither."

—Then, wherefore are ye come ?
    Why watch a worn-out corse ?
Why weep a ripple past
    Down the long stream of force ?
If life be that which keeps
    Each organism whole,
No relic may be traced
    Of what He thought the soul ;
It had its term of passage hither,
But knew no whence, and knows no whither.

    The atoms that were Christ
        Have ta'en new forms and fled ;
    The common sun goes up ;
        The dead are with the dead.
    'Twas but a phantom life
        That seem'd to think and will,
    Evolving self and God
        By some nerve-fashion'd skill ;
That had its day of passage hither,
But knew no whence, and knows no whither.

    If this be all in all ;
        Life, but one mode of force ;
    Law, but the plan which binds
        The sequences in course ;
    All essence, all design
        Shut out from mortal ken :
    —We bow to Nature's fate,
        And drop the style of men !

The summer dust the wind wafts hither
Is not more dead to whence and whither.

 —But if our life be life,
  And thought, and will, and love
 Not vague unrhythmic airs
  That o'er wild harp-strings move ;
 If consciousness be aught
  Of all it seems to be,
 And souls are something more
  Than lights that flash and flee ;
Though dark the road that leads us thither,
The heart must ask its whence and whither.

 To matter or to force
  The All is not confined ;
 Beside the law of things
  Is set the law of mind ;
 One speaks in rock and star,
  And one within the brain,
 In unison at times,
  And then apart again ;
And both in one have brought us hither
That we may know our whence and whither.

 This seeming solid Earth
  We touch through mind alone ;
 These sequences of law
  By the soul's eye are known :—
 With equal voice she tells
  Of what we feel and see

Within these bounds of life,
  And of a life to be ;
Proclaiming One Who brought us hither,
And holds the keys of whence and whither.

  O shrine of God that now
    Must learn itself with awe !
  O heart and soul that move
    Beneath a living law !
  That which seem'd all the rule
    Of Nature, is but part ;
  A larger, deeper lore
    Claims also soul and heart ;
The force that framed and bore us hither
Itself at once is whence and whither.

  We may not hope to read
    Nor comprehend the whole
  Or of the law of things,
    Or of the law of soul :
  Among the eternal stars
    Dim perturbations rise ;
  And all the searchers' search
    Does not exhaust the skies ;
He Who has framed and brought us hither
Holds in His hands the whence and whither.

  He in His science plans
    What no known laws foretell :
  The wandering fires and fix'd
    Alike are miracle :

The common death of all,
   The life renew'd above,
Are both within the scheme
   Of that all-circling Love ;
The seeming chance that cast us hither
Accomplishes His whence and whither.

   What though the types of life
     From their first lowly root
By order'd steps climb up
     To leaf and flower and fruit ;
We ask not why the Hand
     Chose that august advance ;
Content to admire and watch,
     In a wise ignorance.
Life's countless tribes He marshall'd hither ;
We know the Whence, and wait the Whither.

   —Then though the sun go up
     His constant azure way,
God may fulfil His thought
     And bless His world to-day ;
Beside the law of things
     The law of mind enthrone,
And for the hope of all,
     Reveal Himself in One ;
Himself the way that leads us thither,
The All-in-all, the Whence and Whither.

V

FAITH AND SIGHT

IN THE LATTER DAYS

" I prae : sequar."

THOU say'st, '*Take up thy cross,*
   O Man, and follow me :'
The night is black, the feet are slack,
   Yet we would follow Thee.

But O, dear Lord, we cry,
   That we Thy face could see !
Thy blessèd face one moment's space—
   Then might we follow Thee !

Dim tracts of time divide
   Those golden days from me ;
Thy voice comes strange o'er years of change ;
   How can I follow Thee ?

Comes faint and far Thy voice
   From vales of Galilee ;
Thy vision fades in ancient shades :
   How should we follow Thee ?

Unchanging law binds all,
  And Nature all we see :
Thou art a star, far off, too far,
  Too far to follow Thee !

—Ah, sense-bound heart and blind !
  Is nought but what we see ?
Can time undo what once was true ;
  Can we not follow Thee ?

Is what we trace of law
  The whole of God's decree ?
Does our brief span grasp Nature's plan,
  And bid not follow Thee ?

O heavy cross—of faith
  In what we cannot see !
As once of yore, Thyself restore
  And help to follow Thee !

Within our heart of hearts
  In nearest nearness be :
Give Thou the sign ; Say, ' Ye are Mine ',
  Lead, and we follow Thee.

VI

A PSALM OF CREATION

THE Sun lifts his head in his might,
  And climbs the blue steps of the sky ;
Nor stays when he reaches the height,
Nor fears at the setting to die.
For to-morrow again he is born,
To go forth in glory and glee :—
The Sun is Thy creature, O God !
O God, who is like unto Thee !

The Moon, silver ship of the sky,
Rides over the star-dotted blue ;
And the maiden-pure glance of her eye
From the firmament falls like the dew.
The stars round their mistress rejoice,
And sing as her beauty they see :—
These all are Thy creatures, O God !
O God, who is like unto Thee !

The cloud overshadows the vales ;
And the mountain looks down on the cloud ;
The eagle in solitude sails
To the sun o'er the mountain-top proud.

The flood from the thundercloud breaks,
And the torrents roar down to the sea :--
All these are Thy hand-work, O God !
O God, who is like unto Thee !

Then the sky smiles her peace over earth,
And earth her blue smiling returns ;
The lily-bells dance in their mirth,
And the rose in red radiance burns :-
The birds in the forest ring out,
And a thousand wild voices agree.
To praise their Creator and God :
O God, who is like unto Thee !

But higher and fairer than all,
In the counsels of Wisdom and Love
From the dust Thy last work Thou didst call,
Little less than Thine Angels above.
Thou gavest him all to command,
All that wanders on earth or in sea ;
Thine Image Thou gavest to bear :—
O God, who is like unto Thee !

    O Man, from thy bower and home,
The Tree and the garden of Heaven,
By lust and the Serpent o'ercome,
By the sword-glare of Cherubim driven !
Yet, who turn to the Son and believe,
From death by His death to set free
He hath promised ; and He will fulfil :
O God, who is like unto Thee !

VII

THINGS VISIBLE AND INVISIBLE

So far ! so very far !
And this life pressing in, for good and ill,
Sea-like at every pore ; the tangible
Shrunk round the soul with adamantine bar,
—And that world further than the farthest star !

So long ago ! so long !
The world devouring with impassion'd stride
Its history ; Years that rather surge, than glide ;
Peace with her garish triumphs, and the throng
Of wonders working equal weal and wrong ;

Science so free of hand,
Yet vaunting more than she can give or know ;
The dazzling Present with his glory-show ;
—And that scarce-visible life in Syrian land,
Lost and time-buried by the Dead Sea strand !

Strange warfare, which the seen,
The present, wage against the unseen, the past !
As that enchantress, whose sweet guile held fast
Within her palace-walls and forest green
The gray world-wanderer ;—though the faithful Queen

Sate in his island-hall,
And the hearth blazed in winter, and the sun
Shone summer-high above the mountains dun,
As erst before the fatal Spartan call,
And the long siege, and holy Ilion's fall :—

But he remembers nought
Of what has been, and will be :—till the spell
Fade, and his eyes behold the invisible
Long hid :—the faithful wife, the fields he fought
The signs Athena for his safety wrought.

—We too, amid the glare
Of present life, misdeem the world we view,
Our small horizon, for the boundless blue,
Holding all things must be as now they are,
And our experience valid everywhere.

' Let others tell their tale
' Of wonders by the Hellenic questioning mind
' Accepted :—We ne'er saw the shroud unbind
' Its tenant ; nor the cheek change rose for pale,
' Raised up from earth : nor do our powers avail

' To go round Death, and view
' An incorporeal life in realms unseen !
' So let what will be rest with what has been !
' Let the bright Hours their daily dance renew,
' While dreamers chase the Eternal and the True.

' If scanty all we know,
' At least, 'tis knowledge palpable and pure :
We see !—Thus far, our footsteps are secure :
' No more we ask than sense and senses show,
' And Hope and Faith, vain luxuries, forgo.

' The envious Fates on high
' Grudge our horizon, nor will let man stray
' Unpunish'd past the bounds of sentient clay,
' And puff to scorn the adventurers who try
' On self-blown airballs to transcend the sky.

' Man was not made to soar !
' Ascidian-born, not Angel : on this earth
' We clench our sight, nor claim a loftier birth ;
' Accept our fate and creep along the shore,
' And with life's music drown the dead-sea roar.'

—To Circe's sleep-soft isle
Straight let us steer, and live by Circe's creed,
If this be all, if this be all, indeed !
—But should our science of things seen, meanwhile,
Have its own bounds and quicksands : Should the
    smile

Of sceptic doubt assail
The message of the senses ; whether things
Be what we see and touch, or imagings
By self on self imposed, without avail
To make us grasp the Infinite, which our frail

Yet eager reason knows
Essential to the scheme of thought, and yet
Transcending thought, because 'tis infinite :–
If beyond Space and Time no wisdom goes,
—Man's limitations, yet to which man owes

The stage whereon he stands
And breathes and thinks and acts :—How then shall
    man
Cut fragments out from Nature's general plan,
Naming these known, while all beyond he hands
To nescience ?—O fair palace, but on sands,

For all thy bravery, set !—
—To our own selves, O friends, let us be just !
Either not know, or else our knowledge trust :
For all our wisdom, howsoe'er we fret,
Or boast our narrow certainties, is yet

Enframed by hint and guess
And theory :—As when the nights are dark
In Autumn, and men trace a transient arc
That threads its burning way with lightning stress,
And then is swallow'd in blank nothingness,

Deducing from the seen
A credible unseen ; some curve, to roll
Wider for aye, or circle, closed and whole :
—So on our knowledge, partial though, we lean,
And what will be forecast from what has been.

—O sceptics airily bold !
'Tis Reason bids you scorn the facile sneer
That bars the search for truth beyond the sphere !
It is the weak who doubt ; the strong who hold
The resolute Faith where new is one with old.

Within a narrow vale
Rock-wall'd and closed, and skies with cloud o'er-
wrought,
The Powers have planted Man, for life and thought
Knowledge, and love : and, from beyond the pale,
Some bird of God at times above may sail,

Or gleams ascend and go,
As on some castle turret-steps by night
The lamp climbs square by square, and light o'er light ;
And then the shameful things of sin and woe,
The poison-plants that in the valley grow,

The sights that in the heart
Tingle, and make us cry, O Lord ! how long ?
Hast Thou forgotten ?   Why concede such wrong ?
Glare with less luridness, and the cloud in part
Thins, and behind we know Thee, that Thou art ;—

Justice, and Love, and Law
Eternal.—Madness then, aside to thrust
The heart's unsyllabled voice, the instinctive trust,
The signal gleams that lighten and withdraw,
Because with mortal sense man never saw

Nor touch'd nor measured God !–
—As that lone sophist of earth's earlier days
Empedocles, who life's common, sunlit, ways
Scorn'd, and the lava layers of Aetna trod,
And dived for light in Typho's red abode :

Nor saw the Immortals rise
Star-eyed around the zenith, when the veil
Of marsh-white mist parts in the midnight gale ;
Nor where the dawn above horizon lies,
And Phoebus fluting to the saffron skies.

VIII

THE HIDDEN LIFE

THRICE-HAPPY they, who know
 The hidden things of Heaven !
In spirit with the risen Lord
 Who bless'd His sad Eleven :—
Amid the world, within another world,
 Their own unseen, and Christ's, they move,
 And that without seems dark to this
 Sunn'd by the smile of saving Love :—
  Nor will that inner light decline,
  While Thou art ours, and we are Thine.

 The great and gaudy world,
  Throned on his car, goes by ;
Surveys himself, and God, and Earth,
 With self-complacent eye :
Unfolds his liberal lures, and calls mankind
 To share his pleasures, fair and free,
 Low whispering with a mystic smile,
 " If they quit Christ, and worship Me :"
  But all the world we will resign,
  While Thou art ours, and we are Thine.

 Proud Science next, with eyes
 That pierce the heart of things,

The dance of atoms ;—She who darts
  Through space on lightning wings ;
In one vast pattern weaving law with law,
  And Soul alone beyond the plan ;
  With loud and louder voice proclaim'd
  The fount of light and life to Man :
    But all that knowledge we resign,
    While Thou art ours, and we are Thine.

—Ah ! poor external things !
  They only prize ye right
Who, gazing on the invisible Lord,
  Walk in His inner light.
What smiles of gold, what joys of Science high,
  What loveliness of earth below,
  Equals the settled look of Love,
  The peace the world cannot bestow ?
    All, all, with welcome we resign,
    While Thou art ours, and we are Thine !

From fear of death, and that
  Worse fear, that man must go,
Blind puppet of blind force, push'd on
  Through paths he cannot know ;—
From sick despair at ills we cannot cure,
  O Saviour, Thou hast made us free,
  If only on Thy face we look,
  If only we believe in Thee,—
    Safe on Thy bosom to recline,
    While Thou art ours, and we are Thine !

Thrice-happy they, who see
The hidden heavenly home !
Who know He walk'd on earth, and hence
Know He again will come !
O gracious Faith of Reason, sane and sure !
O joy beyond all human speech !
O secret life of peace and love !
Treasure no robber-arm can reach !
—And all in humble hope are mine,
While Thou art ours, and we are Thine.

IX

THE CHURCH OF CHRIST IN ENGLAND

Donec aspiret dies et inclinentur umbrae—

O CHURCH of our fathers in England,
    O Home of the living Lord,
Full fountain of Faith for ages
    And witness firm to the Word !
From Alban, Augustine, and Aidan,
    Paulinus and Cuthbert and Bede,
To our days, ours even, what armies
    Of Christ His long triumph lead !

Saints in lowliness known to Him only ;
    Saints famed in their own despite ;
Life-service pour'd forth for His poor ones,
    Or crown'd with the martyr-light :
Of whom the world was not worthy,
    Counting earth's riches as dross ;
Now laid 'neath gray village spires,
    And the sign of the saving Cross.

The sin-vex'd offspring of Adam,
    While the centuries onward glide,
Have grown in this field of England,
    The tares and the wheat beside :

O visible fold of the Shepherd,
  How oft in His sorrow survey'd,
As the myriad snares of the Tempter
  Himself again have betray'd !

But the Presence unseen at the altar,
  And the Fountain of heavenly birth,
And the Grace of Christ and His Spirit
  Abide with His Church upon earth ;
While the tall cathedral, in brightness
  O'er sin-strife and turmoil below,
Lifts the sign of the great Forgiveness,
  The peace which the world cannot know.

Nor for these alone hath His mercy
  The gracious "Come unto Me " ;
And not of this fold are others
  In secrecy known to Thee !
Grace-led while unknowingly straying,
  Or stumbling in sceptic gloom,
Or dazed by the glare of the Present
  From the Cross and the vacant Tomb.

What then if in ignorant anger,
  Or doing they know not what,
Or casting—unholy alliance !—
  With the infidel legion their lot,
The foes of the Faith in its beauty
  'Gainst the Church of our fathers unite—
But not in our strength, O Saviour !
  Thine only, we gird for the fight.

All wrongfulness, firm yet forgiving,
   For His sake, O brothers, endure :
For His heritage 'tis we are warring,
   And the heritage of His poor :—
Though the spoiler rage hotly around us,
   We stand in full faith in His word ;
For our House on the Rock is founded,
   And the Rock is the Living Lord.

—O Boat on Gennesareth heaving,
   As the winds 'gainst her oarsmen prevail !
Christ's Ark, which the forces of darkness
   In all lands, through all ages, assail !
—The Holy One moves in the tempest ;
   The storm-cries of fury are stay'd :
And lo ! the still Voice of assurance—
   " It is I, Sons ! be not afraid."

X

SURSUM

Vesper adest : iuvenes, consurgite—

ONWARD and upward, whatever the way ;
   Gloomy or glad, through darkness and day :
Vow'd to the end, be it distant or soon,
Under the banner of Christ to march on ;
Strong in His armour to war against ill,
     With a will, with a will,
      Onward and upward !

'Tis to no easy achievement we go ;
Self must meet self, as a man meets his foe ;
Thoughtlessness, indolence, coldness of soul,
Selfishness,—are between us and the goal,
As on life's meadow we war against ill,
     With a will, with a will,
      Onward and upward.

'Tis not the doubters who move us to flight ;
We see in faith, where they waver in night.
'Tis not the evil of things that we fear ;
All the world's mystery cannot be clear
As in this twilight we war against ill,
     With a will, with a will,
      Onward and upward.

But with the self within self, and the heart
Ready to stray, are the pain and the smart :—
Here are the foes, as we march to the goal ;
—Saviour and Lord ! be the soul of the soul
In this hard lifelong campaign against ill,
    With a will, with a will,
        Onward and upward.

Fierce in the heart is the battle of life ;
Bitter the wounds,—yet not hopeless the strife ;
Groans in the darkness, and cry upon cry :
Yet there is One Who will not let us die,
Heading the march as we war against ill,
    With a will, with a will,
        Onward and upward.

High o'er the host floats His banner along,
Red with the love that redeems us from wrong ;
He has made ready a home for His own ;
He will return to the rescue alone,—
Leader and Lord, as we war against ill,
    With a will, with a will,
        Onward and upward !

XI

A PROCESSIONAL HYMN

CHRISTIANS in name and faith,
   As gain we count the loss,
The world's contempt for those who bear
   The banner of the Cross.
Who is on My side? Who with Me?
   The Lord cries day by day :—
In Thy blest service only free,
We range ourselves to follow Thee,
   The Truth, the Life, the Way!

   Then follow, follow, Him Whose blood
     From death and doom hath freed us :—
   The crimson'd footsteps of His love
     To life eternal lead us!

Sons of the Church of Christ,
   A stricter rule we own,
A loftier law, than they who live
   By Nature's law alone.
Thou art our Hope, ascended Lord,
   Our leading-star in Heaven!
But in Thy life with human-kind,
That perfect Manhood here, we find
   Our great Exemplar given.
        Then follow . . .

All justice, truth, and love,
All purity, Thy days ;
We cannot think Thee as Thou wert ;
   We cannot speak Thy praise !
When doubt and danger round us rage,
   Uphold us by Thy power ;
And in Thy mercy lend the grace
By faith to see Thee face to face
   In Death's imperious hour !
            Then follow . . .

  —Ah ! little love to Thee
For Thy great love we bring !
So is there sadness in our song,
   E'en while for joy we sing !
Captain of our salvation, come !
   Uplift Thy victor-sign !
For Thee we fight ; with Thee we bleed :
Lord, to Thy peace Thy soldiers lead,
   And make us wholly Thine !

    Then follow, follow, Him whose blood
      From death and doom hath freed us :
    The crimson'd footsteps of His love
     To life eternal lead us !

XII

MORNING AND EVENING HYMNS

I

L ORD GOD of morning and of night,
We thank thee for thy grace of light :
As in the dawn the shadows fly,
Thy presence shines on us more nigh.

Fresh hopes have waken'd in the heart,
Fresh force to take the loftier part ;
Thy slumber-balms our strength restore
Throughout the day to serve Thee more.

Yet whilst Thy will we would pursue,
Oft what we would we cannot do :
The sun may stand in zenith skies,
But on the soul thick midnight lies.

O Lord of light ! Thy grace alone
Can make the darken'd heart Thine own :
Cleanse then our sin-dimm'd eyes, till they
Unclose on Heaven's eternal Day !

Praise God, our Maker and our Friend ;
Praise Him through time, till time shall end ;
Till psalm and song His name adore
Through Heaven's great day of Evermore,

XIII

II

( ) THOU Who, in Thy night of prayer,
Pain past all pain for man didst bear,
Before Thee now we kneel and pray,
And make confession for the day.

Oft from Thy royal road we part,
Lost in the mazes of the heart :
Our lamps put out, our course forgot,
We seek for God, and find Him not.

What breath of flowers then cheers the night,
What star-eyed heavenly beacon bright?
Thou risest on our way, and we
Find Guide and Path and all in Thee.

When that last sleep and Death are near,
Be Thou with us, Redeemer dear ;
Safe so within Thy fold to wake,
When God's great Judgment-morn shall break.

Praise God, our Maker and our Friend ;
Praise Him through time, till time shall end :
Till psalm and song His name adore
Through Heaven's great day of Evermore.

XIV

III

HIGH in heaven the sun
   Shines his worship to Thee :
The bird in the brightness
   Sings his hymn from the tree :

Thou art praised on the earth,
   Thou art praised in the sky ;
Last comes Thine own creature
   To praise the Most High.

For the sleep, for the waking,
   For the rest of my bed ;
For in Thine arms I slept,
   By Thy touch awakenéd.

As Thou wast in the night,
   Be with me by day :
Morning, noon, evening ;
   All my life, and alway.

Go Thou beside me
   Wherever I go :
Whatever Thou willest,
   Make that I wish it so :

That in thought of Thee
  All I do may be done :
As all great in Thy sight,
  All small in my own.

When to-day brings its trial
  Be Thy voice mine aid :
Say, ' It is I ;
  Be not afraid.

The night is Mine,
  And Mine is the day,
Morning, noon, evening,
  All thy life, and alway.'

XV

IV

THE day is over,
  The darkness is come :
I thank thee, O Lord,
  For the peace of home.

This night and ever
  Keep my feet in Thy way :
Feet slow to follow Thee,
  Feet quick to stray.

Oft wandering from Thee,
  At Thy guidance I chafe ;
Hold Thou me up,
  I shall be safe.

Sad shades of old sin
  Dog my steps as I go :
What was done in the darkness,
  In the daylight I know.

With the voice of the sea
  Sin allures to the brink ;
Stretch out Thine hand :
  Let me not sink.

Whom have I
  In heaven but Thee ?
And on earth there is none
  Set beside Thee may be.

Life soon is over,
  And death will come :
Lord, linger not
  In Thy heaven-home :

As God, come in power
  To judge us and bless :
As Man with man again,
  Come in Thy tenderness.

XVI

FOUR HYMNS FOR PUBLIC USE

I

HYMN FOR INFANT BAPTISM

LORD JESUS, Who didst here Thy love
  With little children share,
With love from highest heaven behold
  And bless this baby fair !
And as we wash with water bright
  Our hands from soil of earth,
So in Thy gracious fountain cleanse
  The stain of human birth.

As that great Ship athwart the flood
  Mankind in safety bore ;
As Israel through the Red-Sea gates
  Foresaw the promised shore ;
As Thou in Jordan river plunged
  Didst sanctify the wave :
So on this child Thy blessing pour,
  All-Merciful !—and save.

O God with Manhood clothed for us,
  Remember Thou the years
Within the Nazaraean home,
  Thine infant smiles and tears :
And by that innocence of Thine
  Do Thou this dear one free

From sin of flesh and sin of soul,
 And make *him* one with Thee !

O safe within Thy sacred Ark,
 The faithful happy fold,
Through all the pain and joy of life,
 The new-born inmate hold !
Guard Thou when gold or pleasure lure,
 Or thoughtless selfish sin,
Or blinding doubt, or black despair,
 And lead the wanderer in.

Safe, safe within the haven hold,
 Whatever storms may rave ;
If long or few the allotted days,
 His ransom'd spirit save ;
So at Thy right-hand may *he* be,
 With those whom Thou shalt own,
On that great Day of Wrath and Love,
 Before the Judgment-Throne.

DOXOLOGY
For each hymn
Eternal Father, Sovran Lord,
 Around, below, above ;
Eternal Son, Who, Man with man,
 Redeem'd the world by love ;
Eternal Spirit, Fount of truth
 And comfort evermore ;
Eternal Trinity, for us
 All mercy we implore.

XVII

II

HYMN FOR HOLY COMMUNION

I T is Thine hour, Ascended Lord !
The holy time is near
With suppliant hands and hearts to kneel
Before Thine altar here.
Creator of the worlds !—As God,
Where Being is, Thou art ;—
Thyself in mystic union now,
As soul to soul, impart.

Ah !—Souls for such a guest unmeet !
Unworthy Thou should'st come,
If Thy pure Spirit breathe not first
To cleanse the sin-stain'd home !
The burden is beyond our strength ;
The thought of it abhorr'd :
Have mercy on us, Son of Man !
Have mercy, risen Lord !

" Come unto Me," we hear Him cry,
With gracious fond request ;
" Come unto Me, world-wearied hearts,
And I will give you rest.

In memory that I died for you,
  To you Myself I give ;
My Body and My Blood are here,
  To take, and eat, and live."

O wondrous Feast, where Christ, beyond
  Our bounded eyesight dim,
In real presence deigns to be,
  And make us one with Him !
One in the Sacrifice that here
  Our inmost hearts adore ;
One with all faithful souls to be,
  And one with all of yore.

With Angels and Archangels now
  We, even we, unite,
To praise Thy Name, Almighty Lord,
  High o'er the highest height.
And by the Blood Thou gav'st for us
  And all mankind to share,
O Son of God, at God's right hand,
  Hear and accept our prayer !

XVIII

III

A MARRIAGE HYMN

O THOU by Whom the life on earth
 Is unforgot on high,
This morn with special blessing sweet,
 O Son of Man, be nigh !
And as Thy glory did not turn
 From Cana's feast away,
Once more as man with men be here,
 And sanctify the day.

What though to mount and desert wild,
 The pensive heart's abode,
Retiring oft,—communion high !—
 Thou wast alone with God :
Yet could'st Thou taste our transient joys,
 The pleasures pure from sin ;
With all-embracing human heart,
 And loving to Thy kin.

—As Isaac in Rebekah found
 The bliss for which he strove ;
As Sarah to her lord gave back
 The comfort of her love ;

As Thine own heart goes eager forth
  To meet Thy cherish'd Bride :
So be the love between these two,
  Till death their days divide.

The joy of helpful toil be theirs,
  The peace of hearth and home :
The single heart, the mutual years,
  The children sweet to come :—
So through life's meadow guide them safe,
  And gently down the slope ;
And bid their eyes the glory see
  Of Heaven's immortal hope.

All flower and fruit of earthly joy,
  All joy when earth is o'er,
Almighty Lord of death and life,
  For these we now implore !
And as they join their faithful hands
  In loving marriage-sign,
Preserve them ever in Thy love,
  Here and hereafter Thine.

XIX

IV
CHRISTIAN BURIAL

DARK gateway of the house of God,
　　Which all Mankind must tread,
A light strikes through thee o'er the graves
　　Of Jesu's faithful dead !
For He has pass'd whose passing through
　　The way for us hath won ;
The Resurrection and the Life
　　Secured by Him alone.

O destined Saviour of the world
　　Before the worlds began,
Thy riven grave and rising brought
　　The hope of hopes to man !
Lord, in that faith we see the day
　　Through death's own midnight shine :—
And resting in that faith to Thee
　　Our dear ones we resign.

Yet 'gainst ourselves, in love's behalf,
　　Our inmost heart will fight :
We clasp them fast, we know not how
　　To let them leave our sight.
The blank of *his* dear face we feel ;
　　The voice beyond recall :

And murmurs 'gainst Thy Will break out,
  And rebel tears will fall.

Ah ! Pardon !—by the crimson drops
  Rain'd o'er Mount Olivet !
Before the downcast eyes of love
  Our sure horizon set ;—
The mortal frame for Heaven renew'd :
  The soul from frailty free ;
The heart within Thy heart received,
  For ever one with Thee.

· Thou hast gone up on high, and left
  Thy shining track afar,
To guide our feet before Thy face,
  And where Thy children are.
Beneath Thy might the stingless darts
  Of Death down-trampled lie :—
The gate of life stands wide for Man :
  Thou hast gone up on high !

DOXOLOGY

Eternal Father, Sovran Lord,
  Around, below, above :
Eternal Son, Who, Man with man,
  Redeem'd the world by love ;
Eternal Spirit, Fount of truth
  And comfort evermore ;
Eternal Trinity, for us
  All mercy we implore.

XX

THE NEW ELEUSIS

(In Memoriam 21 March, 1872)

BABY fair, that know'st not yet
  If the sun be risen or set ;
Know'st not yet of mother's love,
Man on earth, or God above ;
Who thou art, or why we here
Bear this lamb-like burden dear ;—
—Yet the Eternal Counsels hold
All within the holy fold
Thine appointed place, which we
Come in faith to claim for thee.

As the ark that safely bore
Noah the gray billows o'er ;
As the ocean-gates outspread
Before Israel when he fled ;
As, where Jordan waters run,
God to us reveal'd the Son ;
So, His child, thy tender flesh
Takes the saving sign afresh,
Love confirming love bestow'd
When the fount of Calvary flow'd.

Mystic sign of things unseen,
What will be, and what has been !
Things from mortal sense more far,
Yet more true than sun or star !
Mystic Names of Three in One,
That, as age on age has run,
Heard by man in earthly place,
Echo through the spaceless space !
Heaven around the helpless head !
Child in God initiated !

—Mighty Saviour, by Whose hand
Earth was framed as Wisdom plann'd ;
Thou Who cam'st by mortal birth,
Child with children once on earth, —
By the days of Manhood here,
By the vacant sepulchre,
By the glory-seat on high,
By the sudden, speechless cry
Of this suppliant at Thy Throne,
Call our Child Thy very own !

Bid the baby-soul complete
All its birthright promise sweet :
Steadfast faith, emblazon'd sure
On the unfurrow'd forehead pure :
Eyes of hope, and smiles that move
O'er the deep, deep heart of love ·

— O fair dawning, if the light,
Widen on to Heaven's height !
If the flower in Him have root
Who alone gives life and fruit !

Thou, all knowing, well hast known,—
As we kneel before the Throne,
With what ardency of prayer
We give baby to Thy care !
Clasp Thy faithful Arms to hold
This white inmate of the fold ;
Safe through trial-storms of woe,
Snares of sin that smile below,
Safe across life's troublesome sea,
Heaven-haven'd safe with Thee.

XXI

AD ALTARE

ONCE Man with man, now God with God above us,
    Loving us here, and after death to love us :
Enough is this for us, O Saviour dear,
When to Thine altar our faint feet draw near.

'Come unto me all that are heavy laden,
I will refresh you ; mine is love unfading : '
It is enough ; we ask not where Thou art,
Present in space, and in the faithful heart.

—Memorial of the Death, and all it gave us,
Himself offers Himself to cleanse and save us ;
Sacrifice still renew'd, yet still the same,—
The bloodless Lamb, the Cross without the shame.

Once in mean swaddling clothes and infant feature
The world's Creator deign'd to come as Creature ;
So here behind these earthly signs' disguise
The Flesh He took for us in mystery lies.

O ye who named from Christ, should be Christ's wholly,
Mar not the Feast of Love with strife unholy !
Words are too weak that Presence to define,—
Here in Memorial, Sacrifice, and Sign.

So long since Thou wast here, that to our seeming
Thou art like some fair vision seen in dreaming :
With glare and glow and turmoil, sigh and shout,
The world rolls on, and seems to bar Thee out.

Behind the midday sky the stars are shining ;
O shine out on us in our sun's declining :
With loved ones lost, and loved ones yet to quit,
Were this life all, we could not bear with it !

Once Man with man, now God with God above us
Who lov'st us here, and after death wilt love us ;
When to Thine altar our faint feet draw near,
It is enough for us if Thou art here.

XXII

HYMENAEA SACRA

—Graecis et Barbaris debitor sum—

I

INTROIT

F EAR not : come forth : draw near :—Before ye
goes
Immortal Love, with changeless passion pale ;
Star-eyed and crown'd with amaranth and rose,
And flame about him like a marriage-veil :
First-born of Heaven, and messenger of God,
      He signs the golden road.

And Innocence in courage clad is here,
And those well-girdled Graces from on high,
-- Three known in Hellas, and three not less dear
Fair Hope, fair Faith, and fairest Charity ;—
Whilst Angels lifting loud their unheard song,
      Above the altar throng.

--Glide on, fair Visions, glide, with holy Mirth,
Sweet fears, sweet presages of bliss to be,
Love multiplied in love around the hearth,
And Youth exulting in youth's victory ;
Life's triumph in full tide of chasten'd state,
      And joy for words too great.

—But who is He Who to faith's inmost eye
Apart and alien from the glory stands?
Lamb-like and white, as one prepared to die,
The thorn-crown'd forehead and the nail-struck
    hands :
O pitying eyes ! O lips of grief divine !
        What in this hour is Thine ?

—" I, even I, once man with man on earth,
From heaven look down to ratify the vow :—
I feel the touch of holy human mirth ;
The thorns of human love are round My brow :
Thorns blent with blessings for My children true :
        —Approach ! All are for you !

" Pure joys, chaste fires, caressing and caress'd ;
Earth knit with Heaven in mystic union high,
The little faces at the mother's breast ;
On such I look with beatific eye :
Nor any sight dearer to Me than this—
        The heart-deep marriage kiss.

" As Abraham to Sarah set his word,
As Jacob with fair Rachel, so be ye :
As My love is to those who love their Lord
Known or unknown,—yet all beloved by Me :
Through life's dark days to God's immortal year
        So let your love burn clear."

—As silence heard in silence is the Voice,
Yet pure and certain to Faith's secret ear :—
Fear not ! Approach ! 'Tis He who bids rejoice
To Whom His least least little ones are dear :—
One flesh, one soul, one heart, henceforth to dwell ;
      On earth, Immanuel.

HYMN

HOLY Hymen ! whom of yore
    Mortal passion deem'd divine, —
Holy Hymen, we once more
Welcome thee within the shrine :
Holy to the world of old,
Holier we thy presence hold.

—Father of mankind and Head,
Unknown God, and God reveal'd ;
Since man first with woman wed
Thou Thy love dost freely yield
When two hearts, by love made wise,
Offer self in sacrifice.

—Holy Saviour ! Lord on high !
Age o'er age has roll'd and fled
Since Thy blessèd feet went by
On the common earth we tread !
Yet, through long-receding space,
We at Cana see Thy face.

Bring that ancient blessing here
On the home, the board, the bed !
Thou invisible art near ;
Safe their steps hast hither led ;
Lo the feast prepared !—But Thou
Hast kept back the best till now.

—Holy Wisdom, born of Love,
Lead them in Thy tranquil way,
Spread Thy genial wings above,
Shadow in the sultry day :
Shielding them, where'er they go,
From the extremes of wealth and woe :—

Till they gain the shining land,
Mid the twilight guide secure,
Heart in heart, and hand in hand,
Footsteps equable and sure :
While through earth's brief years they prove
All the infinite of Love.

—Holy Love ! that art of God,
Fold them in thine arms, we pray ;
In thine innermost abode,
Two, and one, henceforth for aye :
One on earth, and one above ;
One in everlasting love.

XXIII

THE DAYSTAR

ἀώῖον ἀεροφοίταν
Αστέρα μείναμεν 'Αελίου λευκοπτέρυγα πρόδρομον—

STAR of morn and even,
  Sun of Heaven's heaven,
Saviour high and dear,
Toward us turn Thine ear ;
Through whate'er may come,
Thou canst lead us home.

Though the gloom be grievous,
Those we leant on leave us ;
  Though the coward heart,
  Quit its proper part,
Though the tempter come,
Thou wilt lead us home.

Though the loved and parted
Leave us broken-hearted,
  When o'erwhelm'd we lie
  Look with pitying eye :
Heart of Mercy, come,
Lead us also home.

Saviour pure and holy,
Lover of the lowly,
  Sign us with Thy sign,
  Take our hands in Thine,
  Take our hands and come,
  Lead Thy children home !

Star of morn and even,
Shine on us from Heaven ;
  From Thy glory-throne
  Hear Thy very own !
  Lord and Saviour, come,
  Lead us to our home !

XXIV

A LITANY OF THE NAME OF JESUS

THRICE-Holy Name ! that sweeter sounds
    Than streams which down the valley run,
And tells of more than human love,
    And more than human power, in one :
First from the gracious Herald heard,
    Heard since through all the choirs on high !—
O Child of Mary, Son of God,
    Eternal, hear Thy children's cry !
        While at the blessèd Name we bow,
        Lord Jesus, be among us now !

Within our dim-eyed souls call up
    The vision of Thine earthly years ;
The Mount of the transfigured Form ;
    The Garden of the bitter tears ;
The Cross uprear'd in darkening skies :
    The thorn-wreathed Head ; the bleeding Side ;
And whisper in the heart, " For you,
    For you I left the heavens, and died."
        While at the blessèd Name we bow,
        Lord Jesus, be among us now !

Ah ! with Faith's inward-piercing eye
  The riven rock-hewn bed we see,
Whence Thou in triumph hast gone forth
  By death from death to make us free !
And when on Earth's last awful day
  The Judgment-Seat of God shall shine,
Lift Thou our trembling eyes to read
  In thy dear Face the Mercy-sign.
      While at the blessèd Name we bow,
      Lord Jesus, be among us now !

XXV

A CHRISTMAS LITANY OF CONFESSION

For Music

LORD GOD Almighty on high :
  We have sinn'd in the thought of the heart,
We have sinn'd in the deeds of the hand ;
'Gainst ourselves, against others, our sins
Outnumber the numberless sand :—
    To Thee for pardon we cry,
    Lord God Almighty on high.

Lord God Almighty on high :
  We have wept and repented in vain,
We have broken our promise to Thee ;
Our transgressions roll in like a flood
And are more than the waves of the sea.
    To Thee for pardon we cry,
    Lord God Almighty on high.

Lord God Almighty on high ;
  By the word of the mouth we have sinn'd ;
We have sinn'd by our frown and our smile ;
In our prayers, in Thy House we have sinn'd,
And Thou hast beheld us the while :
    To Thee for mercy we cry,
    Lord God Almighty on high.

Lord God Almighty on high,
　Thy mercy from heaven to earth
　Goes forth ; Thy forgiveness is free :
　Thou hast open'd a refuge for man ;
　Thou hast taken our manhood on Thee :—
　　To Thee with thanksgiving we cry,
　　Lord God Redeemer on high !

Lord God Almighty on high,
　The shepherds have seen as they watch
　The quire of Thine Angels above :
　To all nations the song has gone out
　Of Glory, of Peace, and of Love.
　　To Thee with thanksgiving we cry,
　　Lord God Redeemer on high.

Lord God Almighty on high,
　We come with the shepherds ; we see
　Her of all women most blest,
　As she kneels o'er the cradle, and takes
　That Holy One unto her breast ;
　　To Him with thanksgiving we cry,
　　Almighty Redeemer on high !

Lord God Almighty on high :
　Thou hast come in our flesh ; and to Thee
　Our transgressions, our weakness, are known.
　By Thy Birth, by Thy Life, by Thy Death,
　By Thy right-hand seat on the Throne,
　　Eleison, Christe ! we cry,
　　Almighty Redeemer on high.

XXVI

HYMN TO OUR SAVIOUR

CHRIST Who art above the sky
    Teach me how to live and die !
Thou hast sent me here to be
Born of human-kind like Thee :
Born to walk the flinty road
Which Thy crimson'd footsteps trode ;
Clear mine eyes to track them right,
Leading upwards to the light.

Pure as snow from taint of wrong,
Thou hast known temptation strong ;
Tried and burst the snares that lie
Set to lure us from the sky :
Thou wilt aid me firm to stand
When the tempter is at hand ;
Thou wilt draw my thoughts to Thee,
And the demon-sin will flee.

When I slip, my frailty spare ;
Saviour, save me from despair !
By the mercy-gate Thou art,
Vision of the Bleeding Heart,
Gazing with thorn-circled face
Human-eyed on all the race :

If I kneel before the gate,
Thou wilt never cry " Too late ! "

If in vain my strength has toil'd ;
Hopes defeated ; purpose foil'd ;
If the light of life be dim,
Waning mind, and wither'd limb ;
If my dear ones leave me lone,
Be Thou here when all are gone ;
Thou hast known what anguish is,
Thou canst turn my tears to bliss.

In the day of doubt and gloom,
Let Thy mercy-message come,
O'er my fever'd soul below
Falling soft as snow on snow ;
' Though the mother smile no more
' On the baby that she bore ;
' Bride by bridegroom be forgot,
' Yet will I forsake thee not.'

Though far off in light, by me
Nearer than earth's nearest be :
By the love that brought Thee down ;
By the bitter cross and crown ;
By Thy shepherd-care to save
All Thy flock from font to grave ;
Aid me here to live and die,
Christ Who art above the sky !

XXVII

CHRISTUS CONSOLATOR

Σὺν Χριστῷ—πολλῷ μᾶλλον κρεῖσσον.

HOPE of those that have none other,
Left for life by father, mother,
All their dearest lost or taken,
Only not by Thee forsaken ;
Comfort thou the sad and lonely,
Saviour dear, for Thou canst only.

When hell's legions darken o'er us,
Wiles and smiles of sin before us,
When the wrongs we wrought uncaring
Smite us with the heart's despairing :
Souls in sorrow lost and lonely,
Help us, Lord ! for thou canst only.

By the days of earthly trial,
By Thy friend's foreknown denial,
By Thy cross of bitter anguish,
Leave not Thou Thy lambs to languish :
Fainting in life's desert lonely
Thou canst lead the wanderers only.

Sick with hope deferr'd, or yearning
For the never-now-returning,
When the glooms of grief o'ershade us,
Thou hast known, and Thou wilt aid us !
To Thine own heart take the lonely,
Leaning on Thee, only, only.

XXVIII

THE LOVE OF GOD .

Cras amet qui nunquam amavit ; quique amavit, cras amet.

L ET him love Thee to-day
 Who ne'er loved before ;
And he who loves Thee,
 To-day love Thee more.

Love with mind and heart,
 With body and soul :
Thou gav'st us each part ;
 We should give Thee the whole.

With cheerfulness love Thee
 Age, midlife, and youth ;
With faith and purity,
 Courage and truth :

In health and laughter,
 In sickness and woe :—
But O labour and fear,
 To love Thee so !

Ah Lord, Thou knowest
 Whereof we are made ;
From this burden of love
 We shrink afraid.

Should we love Thee so much,
  What were left behind
For this common life,
  For our human kind?

Should we have enough
  For this world and for Thee ?
—O narrow faith,
  When all is He !

When He loves us first
  From cradle to grave :
—O, love for love
  Is all Thou dost crave !

Thou art not quick
  To mark where we stray ;
Thy voice will lead us
  In love's own way.

Thou shalt cleanse us
  And we shall be clean :
Thou wilt gather
  Thy whole flock in.

Then let him love to-day
  Who ne'er loved Thee before,
And he who loves Thee,
  To-day love Thee more.

XXIX

IN THE VINEYARD

WITHIN a trellised angle idly laid
 'Neath the green lulling shade,
Shunning the toil they hardly care to shun,
 Who waste the priceless hours
 When man's best work is done?

— As from the unsilver'd grass the dawn-dew fled,
 The vineyard's Lord and Head
Call'd in the market-place the stalwart crew
 Of labourers ruddy-brown,
 Pledging each man his due.

Yet,—for God smiled on that full crop, and it
 Was for the vintage fit,—
Again the Lord went forth, and hiring more,
 Sent with their baskets in,
 To pile the purple store.

And now the sudden twilight-pause is near
 When the three stars appear,[1]
Signals of eve and rest from toil retired,—
 While yet the loiterers lie
 Listless, unask'd, unhired.

[1] See Note

But thick the grapes, the mildewing night-air's prey,
　　Be they not stored to-day ;
' More hands, more hearts I crave ; I call ye last,
　　My labourers, Mine, though late,
　　Your day of grace nigh past.'

Ah ! when that loving cry upon them broke,
　　To manhood's part they woke,
Each offering his best strength of heart and limb,
　　And inly only felt
　　The bliss of work for Him !

So these last, till the night when none can toil,
　　Gather the harvest spoil ;
Last these ;—yet when the gate was closed, the Lord
　　Summoning around Him all,
　　Gave them the like reward ;

At the true heart's love-labour, one by one,
　　Rating the service done :- -
Not the world's surface-standard, by success
　　Weighing the man, and blind
　　To the inward more and less.

—The day far spent, yet for my Saviour's sake,
　　Lord ! ere Thine Angels take
The tares and wheat of Earth's last harvest-home,
　　E'en at the eleventh hour
　　May I be call'd, and come !

XXX

LOST AND FOUND

THOUGH we long, in sin-wrought blindness,
From thy gracious paths have stray'd,
Cold to thee and all thy kindness,
Wilful, reckless or afraid ;
Through dim clouds that gather round us
Thou hast sought, and Thou hast found us.

Oft from Thee we veil our faces
Children-like to cheat Thine eyes ;
Sin, and hope to hide the traces ;
From ourselves ourselves disguise :
'Neath the webs enwoven round us
Thy soul-piercing glance hath found us.

Sudden, midst our idle chorus,
O'er our sin Thy thunders roll ;
Death his signal waves before us,
Night and terror take the soul :
Till through double darkness round us
Looks a star,—and Thou hast found us.

O most merciful, most holy,
    Light Thy wanderers on their way ;
Keep us ever Thine, Thine wholly,
    Suffer us no more to stray !
Cloud and storm oft gather round us :
We were lost,—but Thou hast found us.

XXXI

A HYMN OF REPENTANCE

WHEN low on life's horizon, sunk from heaven,
The sun goes down, and night collects on
high,
And grisly shapes of sin, as clouds storm-driven,
In sad procession move against the sky,
Lord, who can bear to die?
But Thou say'st, No;
Not so; not so:—
Though in death's twilight terror take thee,
I will not leave thee or forsake thee.

They pass, the sins of youth, once loved, now loathéd,
In Passion's purple hues and folly dyed;
The sins of age, with leper whiteness clothéd;—
The lust, the lie, the selfishness, the pride:
Who may such sight abide?
But Thou say'st, No;
Not so; not so:
Though dark remorse and shame o'ertake thee,
I will not leave thee or forsake thee.

O Lord and Judge, when from Thy mouth the
 sentence,
Flames, and with prostrate knee and downcast eyes
We sigh before the Throne our late repentance,
 How should the spirit hope for wings to rise
   To Heaven's own Paradise?
    But Thou say'st, No ;
    Not so ; not so ;—
To Him Who bled for man betake thee ;
He will not leave thee or forsake thee.

Thrice-holy Child, Who, pure from pure proceeding,
 By Mary's side in gifts and graces grew ;
Thou Who for our sake once hung pale and bleeding,
 Wilt Thou exact from me the penance due,
   Whose sins Thy death renew?
    But Thou say'st, No ;
    Not so ; not so ;—
Close to My wounded side I take thee ;
I will not leave thee or forsake thee.

XXXII

A LITANY

Κύριε ἐλέησον·
Χριστὲ ἐλέησον.

O LORD GOD eternal,
   The First and the Last,
We are fallen before Thee
As sinners downcast :
Not in anger deal with us ;
Lighten the rod ;
Once more, once more, say
' I am your God : '
   Turn Thy face toward us ;
Put up the sword :
Have mercy upon us,
Have mercy, O Lord !

In the blindness of youth,
In sickness and health,
In the time of trial,
In the trial of wealth ;
As we creep and dwindle
In age away,
In the hour of death,
In the judgment-day ;

Turn Thy face toward us ;
Put up the sword :
Have mercy upon us,
Have mercy, O Lord !

When the lust of wealth
Makes its own self all :
When the pride of strength
Tramples down the small ;
When the world's outcasts
Sit and hide the head ;
When the barefoot children
Cry out for bread ;
  Turn not Thy face from us ;
Draw not the sword :
Have mercy upon us,
Have mercy, O Lord !

When the tempter comes
With gold and smiles,
When the flesh is master,
And thought defiles ;
When faith grows faint
Through pride or fear,
—O Thou that knowest,
Spare us, O spare !
  Turn Thy face toward us ;
Put up the sword :
Have mercy upon us,
Have mercy, O Lord !

By Thy manhood on earth,
By Thy death and life,
By the mountain-peace
And the midnight-strife
By the scourge and cross
And all that pain ;
By Thy golden throne
Set with God to reign ;
   Turn Thy face toward us ;
Put up the sword :
Have mercy upon us,
Have mercy, O Lord !

XXXIII

THROUGH AND THROUGH

Infelix, quis me liberabit?

WE name thy name, O God,
　　As our God call on Thee,
Though the dark heart meantime
　　Far from Thy ways may be.

And we can own Thy law,
　　And we can sing Thy songs,
While the sad inner soul
　　To sin and shame belongs.

On us Thy love may glow,
　　As the pure midday fire
On some foul spot look down ;
　　And yet the mire be mire.

Then spare us not Thy fires,
　　The searching light and pain ;
Burn out our sin ; and, last,
　　With Thy love heal again.

XXXIV

QUIA DILEXIT MULTUM

YES ! She is outcast from the world ;
  The decent crowd of rich and good
With scorn or silence pass her by,
Or bid her search the streets for food :--
Yet when the jewels are made up,
  She shall be ransom'd, yet ;
For she has loved Him more than all,
  And He will not forget.

'Tis not He does not prize the pure,
Or disesteems the holy heart,
Or judges each the same as all,
Or fails to take His liegemen's part :
But that He sees us as we are
  With calm of perfect eyes ;
Reads sorrow hid in reckless mirth,
  And smiles beneath our sighs.

The pitfalls set around the poor,
The impulse of the human blood,
The hunger-hounds that tear the flesh,
Unshared, unfelt, are known of God ;

How very shame disarms the girl ;
　Hell hard by heaven in love,
The babe that the weak hands must feed,—
　Are all confess'd above.

Ah, strange such things on earth should be !
Ah, little arc of the great whole
That our dim eyes can measure here,
Harsh judgments of the happy soul !
The woman's heart in her yet lives,
　And shall be ransom'd, yet ;
For she has loved Him more than all,
　And He will not forget.

XXXV

A HYMN OF PENITENCE

AS a stone my heart, my heart
  To Thee is cold and dry,
Glows not at thought of Heaven,
Nor beats when Thou art nigh.
But if Thy pitying eyes
Upon me Thou dost throw,
The frozen heart melts down,
The founts of sorrow flow :—
    Be near, O Lord, when I
    Before Thy feet confess me !
    I will not let Thee go
    Until Thou bless me.

—O cloud of Self that glooms
Betwixt us and the sky !
O traitor heart that swerves
Where Sin's allurements lie !
In vain Thine instant voice
Warns from the pit to flee ;
A thousand snares invite ;
I turn to them from Thee.

Thine anger cannot move,
Nor do Thy tears distress me :
I cannot pray Thee come
To cleanse and bless me.

—Thou who didst leave to man
Peace, Thy last legacy,
Thy mercy-comfort shed
On me, Lord, even me !
The soul of self cast out,
Subdue the heart of stone,
Seal me on earth for heaven,
Thy child, Thine own ; Thine own !
    — I know Thy presence nigh !
    The wings of Love caress me ;
    Now, now Thou wilt not go
    Before Thou bless me.

XXXVI

THE GARDEN OF GOD

CHRIST in His heavenly garden walks all day,
  And calls to souls upon the world's highway;
Wearied with trifles, maim'd and sick with sin,
Christ by the gate stands, and invites them in.

—' How long, unwise, will ye pursue your woe?
Here from the throne sweet waters ever go :
Here the white lilies shine like stars above :
Here in the red rose burns the face of Love.

' 'Tis not from earthly paths I bid you flee,
But lighter in My ways your feet will be :
'Tis not to summon you from human mirth,
But add a depth and sweetness not of earth.

' Still by the gate I stand as on ye stray :
Turn your steps hither : am not I the Way?
The sun is falling fast ; the night is nigh :
Why will ye wander?   Wherefore will ye die?

' Look on My hands and side, for I am He :
None to the Father cometh, but by Me :
For you I died ; once more I call you home :
I live again for you : My children, come !'

XXXVII

THE CITY OF GOD

δοὺ γὰρ, ἡ βασιλεία τοῦ Θεοῦ ἐντὸς ὑμῶν ἐστ..

O THOU not made with hands,
　Not throned above the skies,
Nor wall'd with shining walls,
Nor framed with stones of price,
　More bright than gold or gem
　God's own Jerusalem !

Not ours the City flash'd
　On that Apostle lone,
Bride-like sent down from Heaven,
　Where God hath set His throne ;
　Where Angels in His praise
　The victory song upraise.

Glorious with white-robed souls,
　That other vision fair
For our sin-weaken'd hearts
　Is all too bright to share ;
　That home of Saints yet lies
　Hid from our longing eyes.

Thou art where'er the proud,
City of God ! bow down ;
Where self itself yields up ;
Where martyrs win their crown ;
　Where faithful souls possess
　Themselves in perfect peace.

Where'er the gentle heart
Finds courage from above ;
Where'er the heart forsook
Warms with the breath of love ;
　Where faith bids fear depart,
　City of God ! thou art.

Where in life's common ways
With cheerful feet we go ;
When in His steps we tread
Who trod the way of woe ;
　Where He is in the heart
　City of God ! thou art.

Not throned above the skies,
Nor golden-wall'd afar,
But where Christ's two or three
In His name gather'd are,
　Be in the midst of them,
　God's own Jerusalem !

XXXVIII

VIRGINI DEIPARAE

M OTHER-MAID all-holy,
  Throned upon thy knee
Evermore th' Almighty
  Child and Lord we see !
While with awe thou gazest
  On the wondrous Face,
Blest among all women,
  Mary full of grace !

—Sung by million millions
  Since the distant day
When she walk'd among us,
  Her sweet stainless way :—
How should we unworthy
  To thy praise draw near ;
How uplift the chorus
  Meet for Heaven to hear?

Of that perfect childhood,
  Of that youthtime fair,
Scarce a whisper lingers
  What thou wast and where :—

Flower amid the flowers
Faith beholds thee go ;
Mystic Rose of Sharon,
Lily pure as snow.

--O'er the holy bosom
She her faithful hands
Folds, in silence waiting
Highest Heaven's commands,
Till the sunbright Angel
Spoke his awful word : --
' Lo ! Thy will is my will,
Handmaid of the Lord.'

Angels and Archangels
Now are round the Maid,
Where the world's Creator
At her knees is laid ;
Where she worships o'er Him,
God and Man in one :—
Son of highest Heaven ;
Mary's royal Son.

By our great first Parent,
(Tempted and beguiled),
We were cast from Eden
To the desert wild :

Second Eve and Mother,
　By the gift she brought
God, through Mary's sorrow,
　Man's salvation wrought.

On the Babe thou smilest,
　He on thee the while :—
But His Father's business
　Calls Him from thy smile.
In the secret archives
　It is writ above
Sevenfold swords shall pierce thee,
　Sevenfold wounds of love.

Who should tell when Mary
　Touch'd the heart of woe ?
When she saw Death's Triumph
　Up the Dool-Way go ?
When the whole world's burden
　Bent Him 'neath the Rood ?
When it shone, to save us,
　With the precious Blood ?

By the Cross now standing
　In that utter woe,
Yet some drops of gladness
　In thy sorrows flow ;

As the loved Disciple
   Reverent leads thee home ;- -
Queen in lowly refuge,
   Heaven's own ante-room !

Now through rest translated
   To the realm assign'd,
Crown'd with grace we greet thee,
   Crown of human-kind !
– Yet, through all the ages,
   Throned upon thy knee
Mother-Maid, th' Almighty
   Child and Lord we see !

XXXIX

A CHRISTMAS HYMN

ON the hillside, where the sheep
White in whiter moonbeams sleep ;
Where with drowsy midnight eyes
His own fold each shepherd spies :
—Why has Night her veil withdrawn ?
Why this dawn before the dawn ?
Who the radiant eager throng,
Chanting forth their glory-song ?
As they gaze in happy fear,
What the hymn the shepherds hear ?

Holy, Holy, Holy,
All Thine Angels cry :
Jesus pure and lowly ;
Jesus throned on high !
Born for us in Bethlehem,
Grant us grace to sing with them
Holy, Holy, Holy !

Brightest Star of stars that blaze,
Whither dost thou bend thy rays?
What the cottage-stable low
Over which thou shinest so ?
Who are these with robe and crown,
Seeking through Ephráta town,

Westward here by wisdom led
Till they kneel and bare the head,
Casting down their gifts before
That star-signall'd gleaming door?

    Holy, Holy, Holy,
    All Thine Angels cry :
    Jesus pure and lowly ;
    Jesus throned on high !
  Born for us in Bethlehem,
  Grant us grace to sing with them
    Holy, Holy, Holy !

By the manger who is He,
Nursling swathed on Mother's knee,
O'er Whom, all amid the kine,
Mary whispers, *Jesu mine !*
—Lamblike there we see Him lie :
Lamb of Heaven for Earth to die ;
Son to God Himself most dear ;—
Very child with children here ;—
Baby nursed on mother's knee,—
—Saviour of mankind—'tis He !

    Holy, Holy, Holy,
    All Thine Angels cry :
    Jesus pure and lowly ;
    Jesus throned on high !
  Born for us in Bethlehem,
  Grant us grace to sing with them
    Holy, Holy, Holy !

XL

ON THE LOVE OF CHILDREN

TO that green hill, the shepherds' haunt,
  Why speed the children's feet?
And who the Youth that sits alone,
The clamorous flock to greet?

His hands are laid above their heads,
Their faces at His knee :
His looks are looks of love ; yet seem
Something beyond to see.

The simple townsmen cross the hill,
And bid the throng away,
' Nor press around the stranger youth,
Nor by the fold delay.'

As one who smiles and wakes, He lifts
A child upon His knee :
' God's kingdom is of such as these ;
So let them come to Me.'

—Ah, Lord and Christ ! Thy perfect heart
No fond excess could touch !
But man's best strength is feebleness,
And we may love too much !

Yet maim'd the man, or poor in blood,
Who glows not with delight
Whene'er the little ones go by
In casual daily sight;

Or when the child at mother's knee,
His altar, lisps a prayer,
And perfect faith, and utter love,
And Christ Himself, is there;

Or when the little hands are clasp'd
To beg some baby grace,
And all the beauty of the dawn
Comes rose-red o'er the face;

Or when some elder one from sport
Her smaller sister wiles,
And two bright heads o'ershade the book;
Half study, and half smiles.

—Ah, Lord and Christ! Thy perfect heart
No fond excess could touch!
Yet when that innocence we see,
How can we love too much?

They twine around our heart of hearts:
Their spell we seek in vain:
Go, ask the linnet why he sings,—
He can but sing again!

To winter-life their bloom and breath
Renew a later spring,
O dewy roses of the dawn,
Fresh from God's gardening !

Earth's treasures waste with use ; but Thine,
O Lord ! by lessening grow ;
From love's pure fount the more we take,
The more the waters flow.

How should we prize the things unseen,
Not prizing what we see ?
How turn away Thy little ones
Without forbidding Thee ?

The Shepherd wills not we should stint
Or count our kisses o'er ;
Nor bids us love His lambs the less,
But Him Who loves them, more.

XLI

A LITTLE CHILD'S HYMN
FOR NIGHT AND MORNING

THOU that once, on mother's knee,
 Wast a little one like me,
When I wake or go to bed
Lay Thy hands about my head ;
Let me feel Thee very near,
Jesus Christ, our Saviour dear.

Be beside me in the light,
Close by me through all the night :
Make me gentle, kind, and true,
Do what I am bid to do ;
Help and cheer me when I fret,
And forgive when I forget.

Once wert Thou in cradle laid,
Baby bright in manger-shade,
By Thy blessèd Mother's care
Shelter'd warm from wintry air :
Now Thou art above the sky ;
Canst thou hear a baby cry?

Thou art nearer when we pray,
Since Thou art so far away ;
Thou my little hymn wilt hear,
Jesus Christ, our Saviour dear,
Thou that once, on mother's knee,
Wast a little one like me.

XLII

A CHILD'S MORNING HYMN

O GOD Who, when the night was deep,
Hast kept me safe and lent me sleep,
Now with Thy sun Thou bid'st me rise,
And look around with older eyes.

Each blessèd morning Thou dost give,
I have one morning less to live :
O help me so this day to spend,
To make me fitter for the end !

O bid all evil wishes fly ;
The fretful word, the careless eye ;
Aid me to think, in all I do,
'God sees me : would He have it so?'

Make my first wish and thought to be
For others sooner than for me ;
And let me pardon them, as I
Hope for God's pardon when I die.

Be with me when I work and play ;
Be with me now and every day,
Be near me, when I pray Thee hear ;
And when I pray not, Lord ! be near.

XLIII

A CHILD'S EVENING HYMN

O LORD Who, when Thy cross was nigh,
    Didst wake and pray as night went by,
Thy gentle sleep like dew once more
Upon my head I pray Thee pour.

One little heap of days for me
Is measured out by God's decree ;
And one day from that little heap
Is gone as I lie down to sleep.

And I know not how soon the tale
Of my few days and short may fail : —
O God, whene'er !—for Thy dear Son,
Me, even me, have mercy on !

O strange, that as I kneel and pray,
He from His throne hears all I say !
—Give me but what for me is best :—
This is enough : Thou know'st the rest.

O sleepless Shepherd of the sheep,
Now fold me in, and bid me sleep :
From evil safe, and night's alarms,
Nursed in Thine everlasting arms.

XLIV

THAT CHILDREN SHOULD BE GENTLE

For School use

HOW sad the strife and storm that rise
When angry thoughts breed angry cries !
But quiet song and gentle word
Should only from our lips be heard.
　We'll remember all the week,
　Softly sing, and gently speak.

We know when Christ our Lord was young,
No angry word e'er cross'd His tongue :
And when He grew no more a child,
His voice was loving, soft, and mild.
　So should we be mild and meek ;
　Softly sing, and gently speak.

But we have other duties too ;
Not only must we speak, but do :
And gentle hands and quiet feet
For little children's ways are meet.
　We should practise what we know ;
　Softly step, and gently go.

Our Saviour's ways thus best we keep,
For lovingly He led His sheep ;
And when His foes were raging by,
He gently gave Himself to die.
  We should here His likeness show ;
  Softly speak, and gently go.

XLV

AN INCIDENT AT MENDRISIO

April 23, 1886

' Ἄφετε τὰ παιδία ἔρχεσθαι πρός Με—

IT was the Day, the sad, the good,
   The Day thrice-blest, when He,
The Love uniting God with Man,
   Hung on the Tree :—

And where within the transept wide
   A vacant space was made,
With reverent touch the village hands
   His Image laid ;

Not such as old Donato wrought :
   Yet this rude craftsman's heart
With deeper passion stamp'd the wood
   Than finer art.

And all the Italian throng was there,
   Bronze-wrinkled crone, and maid,
Fathers with sons ; the lame, the blind,
   Where Christ was laid.

They knelt for prayer ; they kiss'd for love
Their Saviour's riven Side,
The Hands, the Feet, the bleeding Heart
For us Who died.

But in the throng what part has she,
The little maiden sweet,
Who climbs and trembles to the Cross
With fervent feet?

Like her, the Blesséd Virgin Child
Who clomb the Temple-stair,
God-given, given back to God,
Pure, sacred, fair.

—With kisses fast and close, herself
Upon the Face she throws ;
The innocent breath with love is warm,
Sweet as the rose.

Ah, darling ! though thine infant heart
Outrun thy knowledge dim,
E'en on God's throne that eager love
Is dear to Him.

XLVI

GUARDIAN ANGELS

THE myriad Angel hosts, whose glance
  The things unseen surveys,
Each o'er the heart he has in charge
  Bends down with loving gaze.

He may not break the natural bar
  That veils the world above :
As summer breeze on summer corn,
  The soul he sways with love.

Invisible guardians at our side,—
  When Satan's smiles allure,
Man's ear and eye, sin's treacherous gates,
  'Gainst sin they hold secure.

They guide the vagrant tongue aright,
  They check our heedless mirth ;
With comfort the weak-hearted stay,
  The fallen lift from earth.

Ah ! Yet the lucent Birds of God,
  These star-crown'd sinless Powers,
Sharp pangs of human grief must pierce,
  E'en in their heavenly bowers :

1

The frailty of entrusted souls ;
The children driven astray ;
The pitfalls lurking round mankind ;
The maidens cast away :—

O they must veil their Angel eyes
From earth's dark hell of shame !
The perjured lips, the blood-mark'd hands,
The sins without a name !

' Lord Jesus, to Thy fold,' they cry,
' Restore Thine erring sheep ; '
And weep Love's pitying tears for us,
Because we do not weep.

XLVII

THE KING'S MESSENGER

H E goes in silence through the crowd ;
   A veil is o'er his face ;
Yet where but once his eyes are turn'd
   There is an empty space.
The whispering throngs divide and stir :
'Tis he ! 'tis the King's Messenger !

 We may perforce buy off the thought.
   Or stifle or ignore :
The day at last will come on us
   When day will come no more :
When on the spaces of the sky
We hardly lift a wearied eye :

When rising death-mists change and blot
   Familiar features near :
When we can give nor word nor sign,
   Nor what they utter hear ;
When mother's tears no more are shed
For little faces round the bed ;

When Science folds her hands and sighs,
  And cannot bridge the abyss ;
And That, which once seem'd life, seems nought
  Before the enormous This ;
All days, all deeds, all passions past
Shrunk to a pin's point in the vast :—·

Then face to face to meet the King
  Behind His messenger !
—O could we see that hour go by
  Whilst youthful pulses stir,
With all our future to forgive,
We scarce could bear the sight, and live !

—Thou Who for us hast suffer'd death,
  Remember we are men ;
Thou on the right hand of the Throne,
  Have mercy on us then ;
Thou from the King our pardon bear,
And be Thyself His messenger.

XLVIII

DEATH AND THE FEAR OF IT

L ORD ! How fast the minutes fly
 'Twixt us and the hour we die !
Days are weeks before we know :
Weeks to months untimely grow ;
And behind each glad New Year
Death his ambush sets more near.

Death ! by whomsoever heard,
'Mongst all words most fearful word !
  Quit each thing familiar here !
Face to face with God appear !
Change no mortal tongue can tell :-
All's in that one syllable !

Hour of dread farewells to be !
Faces more than life to me ;
Little lips that beg me stay ;
Tears I shall not wipe away ;
Faithful hand, yet clasp'd in mine :-
Death Triumphant ! all is thine !

Author of man's mystic lot,
God, Thy ways as ours are not :
Thou hast destined us to be
Seized by death, yet safe in Thee :
Love Immortal casting out
Feverish fear, and freezing doubt.

—In the spaces of the night,
In the depths of dim affright,
Jesus, with our trials tried,
Do not Thou forsake my side !
Childlike on Thy faithful breast
Hold my heart, and bid me rest.

Like a sword above my head
Death is hanging by a thread ;
Yet, O gracious Lord on high,
Surely Thou wilt hear my cry,
By Thy life laid down for me
Turning death to victory !

Only this can light the grave,
Thou hast died :— and Thou wilt save :——
Thou by lying low in earth
Hast assured our second birth,
Bidding in the sunless tomb
Amaranthine roses bloom.

If the spirit shivering shrink
From annihilation's brink,
Through the soul like sunshine come,
—' Death is but another womb :
Born through woe to human breath,
Ye are born to God through death.'

—Nearer than the nearest by,
Be beside me when I die !
With Thy strength my weakness nerve
Ne'er through fear from faith to swerve ;
So, Death's storm-vex'd portal past,
Safe in Thee to sleep at last.

XLIX

R. I. P.

30 September, 1883

IF 'tis Thy will my years outrun
   The love from boyhood unestranged,
   By all his changeful lot unchanged,
The Brother's heart with mine at one,

Thy comfort, Lord, vouchsafe at last :—
   Not such as bids us now forget
   The love that from our skies has set,
Or blurs the memory of the past.

If 'tis Thy will that we, whose feet
   Earth's twilight pathways breathe and tread,
   Should pray Thy mercy for the dead
And lightening of the penance meet

For frailties of the fallen race,—
   O Son of Mary, let the cry
   Because he loved much—heard on high,
E'en from a sinner, find Thy grace !

If 'tis Thy will that Spirits above
  With exiles of the earth may feel,
  And thought to thought itself reveal
—O let not my remorseful love

Beat idly 'gainst the golden gate,
  Nor he the pardon sought withhold
  For word unkind, repulses cold ;
Nor count these useless tears too late !

If 'tis Thy will that, 'neath the Throne,
  The souls who truly loved on earth,
  Transfigured through Death's second birth,
Shall meet and gaze and own their own,

Rosed o'er with Love's ethereal fire—
  Star-like that face on me will shine,
  O loved and lost, O Brother mine,
Fulfilling so the heart's desire.

L

DESIDERATISSIMAE

WHILE in Solitude's inward cell
　　All amidst the crowd I dwell ;
Ply life's little part, and take
Each task up for Thy dear sake,
Thoughts of all Thou wast and art
Pierce yet soothe the bleeding heart ;
And those upward footsteps teach
My faint feet Thy path to reach :—

Path to where, with all who died
Clinging to the Crucified,
Thy sweet songs adoring rise,
Saint mid Saints in Paradise.
Still beneath Thy faithful care,
Ah ! might I the Vision share !
Love Thee none the less, but more,
Heart with heart, the Lamb adore !

Yet meanwhile I would not Thou
Should'st behold what I am now :
Trembling lest this sin-struck heart
Me from Heaven and Thee should part.

If Thou seest my earthly way,
For the soul in prison pray ;
Soul by Satan's treachery tried ;
Sure, thou wilt not be denied !

—Lord, who in Thy wounded side
Bid'st the heavy-laden hide,
Though the sun of life be set,
Through the darkness aid me yet ;
Patient down the way of woe
Grant me in Thy steps to go ;
My fond tears forgive, accept ;
Thou art Man ; and Thou hast wept.

LI

I AM THE RESURRECTION AND THE LIFE

DARK World, rejoice ! The day-spring
　　Has broke, more bright than when
The star-crown'd Angel chorus
　　Sang God's good news to men,
　　The Lord of Life e'en now
　　　From Death's dim prison
　　　This third day risen,
　　With victory on His brow
　　　　　　Risen !

O day that seal'd for ever
　　The hope of hopes to man !
Made Death himself the gateway
　　To life's immortal span !
　　That brimm'd with quickening light
　　　The soul's grave-prison,
　　　Whence He had risen,
　　God's Daystar in His might
　　　　　　Risen !

For all the million millions
 Whirl'd on this roving ball
Since man's creation-morning,
  One Lord hath died, for all ;
   God, yet still Man, He springs
   From Death's dim prison,
   In glory risen,
   With healing on His wings
    Risen !

But most who mourn their dearest
 Through desolate silent years,
Loved with what utter longing,
  And wept for with what tears—
   For them the Love that died
   Unbars life's prison :—
   They see Christ risen,
   The loved ones at His side—
    Risen !

EPITAPHS

I

ON A LITTLE CHILD

1867

PURE, sweet and fair, ere Thou could'st taste of ill
God will'd it, and Thy baby breath was still.
Now 'mong His lambs thou liv'st thy Saviour's care,
For ever as thou wast, pure, sweet and fair.

II

ON AN INFANT

14 July—1 August, 1870

OUR little lamb He lent awhile,
Pure as Himself from stain ;
Then said ' My kingdom is of such,'
And call'd it home again.

III

ON A MOTHER

1869

ANCHOR of many hearts and joy of all,
Too soon for us she heard the Master's call :
Ah ! for us all too soon ; but not for her ;
Our comfort, she ; but He, her Comforter.
For when to death her spirit gently bow'd,
And the heart's sunshine went beneath the cloud,
And in her smile the light of love grew dim,
She fell asleep in God ; and is with Him.

IV

IN MEMORIAM

FRED. PARRY HODGES

27 October, 1880 ; Lyme Regis

NIGH fifty years he served the allotted flock,
And from earth's pastures led them to the
Rock,
And guided where the living waters run,
God's gift to man through His ascended Son.
True, generous, kind, he lived the Faith he taught ;
Preach'd in his deeds, and by example wrought.
With us he pray'd, and for us :   and now we
Pray that with him our After-death may be.

V

IN MEMORIAM

W. F. HOOK

20 October, 1875

TO some, the conqueror's crown, the patriot's fame,
The one achievement which creates a name ;
And, had he cared to shine in human eyes,
He who lies here had but to claim his prize ;
In God's good gifts so rich, he might have gain'd
Whate'er Ambition schemed, or Fancy feign'd.
But now - since others' joy, and others' smart,
Lay nearer than himself to that great heart,
And, finding glory dross, and life a day,
For others' lives he gave his own away,
With the forgotten casting-in his lot——
O yet his name is, elsewhere, unforgot !
High mid His faithful ones in Christ's own fold,
And in the Eternal Memory enroll'd.

VARIA

K

I

PAUSANIAS AND CLEONICE

AN OLD-HELLENIC BALLAD

Argument

PAUSANIAS, Regent of Sparta, after commanding his coun-
trymen in the victory of Plataea, was corrupted by sight
of Persian luxury and despotism, and began to act the
tyrant, notably in his conduct to a free maiden of Byzantium, where he was in command of the Greeks allied
against the King of Persia. They, disgusted, withdrew
from him, who, meanwhile, tormented by the shade of the
maiden, whom he had slain in error, after vain efforts to
appease the spirit, was recalled to Sparta. His treason-
able offers to Persia being now betrayed by a slave, he
was starved to death by order of the citizens in the Brazen
House of Athena.
These events fell between 479 and 466 B.C.

I

B Y the wine-dark Euxine sea,
　　Where Second Rome once lifted high
Her pomp of marble majesty,
An earlier city clothes itself in glee.
—Megarian Byzance !—for Plataea's plain
　　　Soaks with Persian gore ;
　　　Hellas breathes once more ;
Pausanias' arm has won ; the land is free again.

II

Let the triumph then flame out
Along her terraces and towers,
The curved sea-wall, the cypress bowers,
In lights and altar-fires and song and shout :
For golden-panoplied Masistes lies
    Naked 'mong the dead !
    Artabazus fled !
Pausanias' name goes up in hymn and sacrifice.

III

Peace in all her sweetness hail !
No more the clarions ravish sleep ;
Red rust-stains o'er the lances creep ;
Gray spider-meshes gather on the mail :
Glad youths with girls the Comus-carols share ;
    In our feastful bowers
    Song puts forth her flowers :
Peace with thy children, hail ! Hail, Wealth and
    Order fair ! [1]

IV

Why, with envy of his name,
Should Spartan hands the tale erase
From the tall Delphic tripod-base ?
—The day was thine,- and thine must be the fame !
Pure hero, brave and pure, for such alone
    God with glory crowns ;
    Bulwark of our towns,
Byzantium welcomes thee, and calls thee now her own !

[1] See Note

K 2

V

—Vain the welcome and the praise !
Unconscious irony of man !
Not knowing how the God His plan
By evil tools works out, and hidden ways :
For He with lightning eyes the secret heart
      Searches through, while we
      Guess from what we see,
And coarsely, by success, define the hero's part.

VI

Sparta's life and lore forgot,
He that was once Pausanias, now
Before the King he smote can bow,
Swine-changed as Circe's herd, and knows it not !
Traitor to Hellas and Heraclid name,
      Despot, in his lust
      Hardening, to the dust
Men, women, all, he hurls, the victims of his shame.

VII

—Fairest of Byzantine maids,
Fair Cleonicé, pure and sweet,
With downcast eyes and modest feet
Moving as Leto through Gortynian glades :
Heart of thy mother's heart from infant years
      As the gentle face
      Rounds to maiden grace,
And she through very love thy beauty sees with tears.

VIII

As the dearest nymph of all
Who bend round Artemis in the dance,
When eyes with star-like rapture glance,
And silken waves on ivory shoulders fall,
Lips part for joy, not breath,—she stands upright,
    Like the Delian palm,
    In her maiden calm,
Whilst all the air around trembles with beauty's light :

IX

—For thy mother best, and thee,
If thy last breath had been the first !
This day the tyrant's greedful thirst
For his foul harem claims thy purity :
Sure sign of baseness at the heart, he deems
    Woman slave and toy ;
    Cast aside, when joy
Sickens the sated sense ;   forgot with morning dreams.

X

Midnight as a robber's mask
Now muffles close o'er town and sea :
Now force and fraud and sin are free
To lurk and prowl and do their wolvish task :
Now tow'rd the tyrant's spear-encircled bed,
    Tow'rd Pausanias' tent,
    Lo, white footsteps bent,
So shame-struck soft, her heart speaks louder than her
    tread !

XI

Helpless, hapless victim-maid !
Not first nor last, I ween, art thou,
Thy gentleness coerced to bow,
Losing thyself to lust,—and nothing said !
Only a girl ! only one more, abased,
    While man's tyrant-might
    Boasts thee frail and light,
And thy creation mars, to his desires disgraced !

XII

Now the brutal couch she seeks
Through blinding night—for, at her prayer,
The odorous lights extinguish'd are—
To hide from self her horror-kindled cheeks :
Ghost-like with vagrant steps she threads the camp :—
    Labyrinth-like the shade
    Of that tent :— the Maid
Strikes down with clanging fall the lightless golden
    lamp.

XIII

Sudden from the darkness wide
As some blue trenchant lightning-flame
That seams the cloud, a scimitar came,
And Cleonicé by Pausanias died !—
Dead !—for the traitor deem'd himself betray'd !
    Dead !—The Persian sword,
    Slavery's sign abhorr'd,
From worse than death, by death redeem'd the Dorian
    maid.

XIV

Morning comes ; and with the mo,
The timely bird, the clarion-cry,
The crowding sailors' glad ' Hy—hy,'
The jostling galleys in the sun-gilt Horn :
But all the happy music of the day
     O'er her went in vain,
     Where upon the plain
Like some young palm, in all its promise fell'd, she
     lay.

XV

Morning comes : And he who wrought
The shame, as one refresh'd awakes,
And lust's remorseless counsel takes,
And names another victim in his thought ;
' But if our citizens fret, and 'gainst my sway
     With the allies combine,—
     Persia's King is mine !
Europe to Asia yoked shall soon my will obey ! '

XVI

' Go where blinded Insolence
And selfish Lust, her child, lead on ! '—
O voiceless Voice, to him alone
Whisper'd within, unfelt by mortal sense !
Aye whisper'd ! And a Presence now is by ;
     Ever at his side
     Seems unseen to glide ;
A clinging second self ; a Shade he cannot fly.

XVII

As the fever-feeble wretch,
With lidless eyes and stirless head
Sees a gray ghost beside his bed,
And in the vision knows his fated Fetch :
Or gaunt Orestes, when the deed was done,
    Queen and co-mate slain,
    Full requital ta'en,
Winning his game, himself found by the Furies won ; [1]

XVIII

In his ears the frenzying song,
That chain'd the soul and dried the flesh,
And flung a close air-woven mesh
Around its prey, while wingless serpents throng
Draining him to a shadow ; and his brain
    Maddens with the sting,
    As the Erinnyes sing
The songless chaunt of Hell, the soul-corroding strain.

XIX

Yet the Loxian gave him peace !
And to the Hill of War the fair
Athena bade the youth repair,
And purged his guilt, and voted him release ;
For he repented of parental gore,
    Of that double stroke ;
    And the Just Ones' yoke
Was lighten'd from his neck, and he breathed free
    once more.

[1] See Note

XX

—But the God-abandon'd chief,
By his own passions lash'd and whirl'd,
To deeper depths each day was hurl'd,
Yet from that haunting Voice found no relief :—
' Where Insolence and Lust drive down their prey,
   Go, Pausanias, go !'
   —Doom'd to sink more low
Then e'er his glory soar'd, on red Plataea's day.

XXI

Sparta, from his place of pride
Reclaims her King : he must obey !
Through wild Arcadia runs the way,
Arcadia, land of song and mountain-side ;
Where Phoebus o'er his favourite valley reigns,
   Bassae green and deep ;
   And white columns peep
Nymph-like amid the trees, fairest of Grecian fanes.

XXII

There athwart the rock-wall white
The long fir-files their spires lift,
Upclimbing dark from rift to rift,
Till snow and azure crown the dazing height ;
There, as Pan sleeps below the zenith sun,
   Silence only stirs
   Where the grasshoppers
Chirr their dry chaunt, and streams with summer
   music run.

XXIII

O'er the vale the Mount of Light,
Lycaeus, lifts his holy head,
One shadeless silver pyramid,
O'ertowering Hellas with Olympian height :
There, Neda and Theosöa, nymphs divine,
    Nursed the rocks among
    Zeus, when earth was young ;
And yet the Lord of Lords finds here his best-loved
    shrine.

XXIV

Pure in heart and conscience-whole
O they should be, who dare to come
Within dread Nature's secret home,
And nought 'twixt us and her to mask the soul !
As the proud despot treads the vale alone
    Fiercer in his ear
    Burn the words of fear,
And all that ambient air is Cleonicé's moan !

XXV

Whither from this gad-fly sting,
This coward-making conscience fly ?
—He sees Phigalia's rampart high,
And Neda flowing from her mountain-spring
Past Lycosura ;—There, as legends said,
    Huge Lycaeus hides
    In his rifted sides
The Callers-forth of Souls ; the Summoners of the
    Dead.

XXVI

Eastward up the vale he turns,
Where walls of rock to left and right
Flicker with living tapestry light,
Aconite, and green mist of feathery ferns :
There, jasmine-stars and golden cistus beam,
    While the waves below
    Pearl and sapphire flow,
Deepening their voice, as near their birthplace still
  they stream.

XXVII

Rushing waters, could ye not
Far sea-ward bear the damning cry ?---
But now the journey's goal is nigh,
Where one dark pool marks out the fountain-spot :
With lichen-gilded layers and splinter'd steep
    Arching high and wide,
    Springs the mountain-side,
And the black mirror lies in marble stillness deep.

XXVIII

Sad, as one himself compell'd
The spirits to compel, uprear'd
His grayness the Soul-summoner weird,
And pray'd, and by the hands Pausanias held,
Bending him o'er the mirror blank, and said
    ' In the Absolver bold,
    Whom thou wouldst behold
Name in thine heart ; nor wilt thou vainly seek the
  dead.'

XXIX

Shuddering o'er the shuddering pool,
He sees the Face, not maiden-bright,
But ring'd with blue unhappy light,
And, starting, gazed around, and called her :—Fool !
For she, not here, but where pure souls abide
    In the eternal day,
    Innocently gay,
Is what she was on earth, transfused and glorified.

XXX

Fled the vision : and alone,
— As when the storm-clouds leeward-go,
Faint flashes broad and reddening glow,
And far horizons mutter undertone,—
These words around the cavern flit, no more,
    ' Hence to Sparta flee ;
    There, release will be : '
And, as he stood, the rock and waters flared with
    gore.

XXXI

' Fly ! ' the Soul-evoker cried,
' The God has spoken !   Only, know
His message sounds for weal or woe
As the heart is, or is not, purified :
The Soul is its own Fate.'   Pausanias groan'd,
    Frown'd, and groan'd again :
    —'Twas one moment's pain !
Pride's icy heart grew big ; the guilt was unatoned !

XXXII

Therefore, O just Gods below,
When hollow Sparta he retrod,
Ye smote him with your Fury-rod
That smites but once, and needs no second blow !
For lust breeds lust, treasons on treasons call,
    Till a servile mouth
    Tells the shameful truth :
Plataea's victor now is Persia's friend and thrall.

XXXIII

By the temple brazen-wrought
Lo ! his own mother's hands begin
To pile the stone and wall him in,
Captive to famine, where he safety sought.
Unhappy Chief! traitor to God and Greece.
    Now on Spartan ground
    He the end hath found !
But only where thou art, Cleonicé, there is peace.

II

TO MY MOTHER'S MEMORY

SO many years are gone since last I saw thee,
  And I, alas ! so young
When that black hour its shadow o'er me flung,
That but with feeble tints,
Vague strokes, half lights, time-troubled tints,
E'en to the inner eye my heart can draw thee.
Yet sometime memory wakes,—
O ! not in night, or sadness, but when dawn
Slopes all her silver o'er the dewy lawn,
Or golden day dimples on mountain-lakes,
Or evening's wild-dove tolls her brooding strain,—
Then I remember me of what thou wast,
And see thee once again.

Though denizen'd so long in far-off bowers
  And in another air,
  Her form I know 'mong all the blest ones there.
  Before toward me she turns,
  My gazing heart within me burns,
  And a new rose-flush flames through all the flowers.
  I know the step, the dress,
  The grace around her way like sunbeams shed ;
  The worshipp'd hand, on my then-golden head

Laid with the touch of utter gentleness ;
The hair—but O ! no more what it had been,
Silver'd with pain, not age—but fair as once
In youth, by me unseen.

'Mong all the bright ones there is none such other !
   Clear through that myriad throng
   Like some sweet subtle scent I catch her song :—
   O by whatever name
   Now named, thy child, my part I claim ;
My soul goes forth to thee : I call thee, Mother !
   Smile the low serious smile
   Which animated youth to highest aims :
   Lay thy soft hand upon the fever flames
   That manhood's brain to foolishness beguile :
   Hold me once more upon the faithful breast :
   Kiss my life-wearied eyelids, say, *My Child !*
   And then I shall find rest.

As when a dove from her soft flight alighting
   More softly glides along,
   Her feet float by me mid the rose-crown'd throng ;
   With eyes as if of one
   Who sees, and sees not, and is gone
Where other eyes allure, and hands inviting.
   —Hast thou no word for me ?
   None for me, Mother, never needing more
   The wisdom needless on the golden floor,

The counsels of thy bright sobriety?
—Or, musing on the man that once was child,
Canst not endure to look on all this change ;
So fair,—now so defiled?

Mid all the white-robed flock of God, that slowly
    Stream up the heavenly ways,
I see the star above her forehead blaze
    When she bends back, (as they
    Who, turning from their height, survey
Some low dim spire to far remembrance holy) ;
    And, flash'd from breast to breast,
A voice rings clear, as when, knee press'd on knee
And face on face, her whisper'd words to me
Were as the words of God ;—and this unrest
Of later years through all the nerves is still'd,
Like some stream-tortured pool, that calms at once
    With level crystal fill'd.

Then she : ' When once we reach the great releasing,
    ' Not only are we freed
    ' From all that clogs the soul, all earthly greed ;
    ' But also pain and fear
    ' Leave the transnatured spirit clear,
    ' And hope, in her fulfilment, finds her ceasing.
    ' Whilst here I watch their way
    ' Whose life, in life, was more to me than life,
    ' The chaunt of peace streams from the heart of
        strife ;

'And all that seems but wrong and disarray
'Is harmonized to beauty and to good ;
'All thou deem'st pain and ill, in God's high scheme
'Is love misunderstood.

' Poor human souls, each in its earth-framed prison,
  ' The separate fleshly cell,
  ' That meet, but cannot touch, whilst there they
    dwell !
  ' Here I, my child, with you
  ' Have real oneness, union true ;
' Eyes never dimm'd by tears, and stainless vision.
  ' Love, by the central Throne,
  ' Before time was, for this took up his seat,
  ' That heart in heart, and soul in soul, should beat,
  ' That One should be in All, and All in One :
—' So here I bide among the rose-crown'd throng
  ' Waiting Love's day, and mine, and thine, and thee :
  ' For it will not be long.'

I heard : and face to face she seem'd before me,
  And moved her hand toward mine.
  And I : 'Tis so ! now let me take the sign ;
  With tears and kisses hold
  The slender fingers kiss'd of old ;—
  But silent, flowerlike, she leant back, and o'er me
  Her hand, as blessing, held ;
  And aweful love was on her eyelids spread,
  And the pure pearly star, that crown'd her head,

Flash'd sudden rose : and my wild heart was quell'd.
And now she turn'd : and, in her turning, Love
Was heard ;—Then bent her steps through Heaven ;
  — for she
Knows all the ways thereof.

Go, Song ! poor satisfaction of large debt
  Which that fair Saint on me for life has bound :
  And if the wise thy reason seek,
  Say, Thou hast been long sought, and lately found ;
  My blame, if far below her excellence ;—
  The spirit is willing, but the tongue is weak.

III

IN MEMORY OF ROBERT BROWNING

(At 29, De Vere Gardens
28 December, 1889)

TWILIGHT and peace in the chamber;
    Twilight of death and peace
For him who the strife, the long battle of life,
    Had fought out to the last release :

Dead in a dying city,
    Through her silent water-ways sped
Toward the misty West, and the place of rest
    And gray home of the mighty dead :

Now bathed in silence and twilight
    Where with wisdom's roseate glow,
Quick lightnings of wit, the chamber was lit
    So lately,—yet so long ago :

Where eyes that from youth ne'er look'd on me
    But the heart's bright message they bore,
The welcoming lip, the hand's honest grip,
    Were mine—mine now never more :—

There with amaranth cross and bay-wreath,
    Inane munus, I strove,
Knelt there and pray'd where they said he was laid
    To do the last office of love ;

Love reverent, grateful, deep,
  For the treasure that only they,
The poets of love, the wise from Above,
  To the world in its deadness convey :

For he, Star-crested, Hope-armour'd,
  Struck straight at a swelling tide ;
In the valley of doubt, with clarion shout,
  Chased coward and doubter aside.

Then the vanish'd Presence in brightness
  Was felt once more in the room,
While the worn-out shred the great spirit had shed
  Lay garnish'd and still for the tomb.

Not there was the soul I had loved,
  Where the mortal raiment was laid,—
Death's vanishing spoil, the lamp without oil,
  Blank sheath of the God-wrought blade,—

Bare walls of man's house, where no fire
  On the central hearth-stone glows !—
Till silently round me a vapour of sound,
  The music of memory, rose :—

And *Blest are the dead in the Lord;*
  For they rest from their labours, I heard ;
With a *Love is best !*—and the life now at rest
  Was summ'd in that one brief word.

IV

F. C. C.

6 MAY, 1882

FAIR Soul, who in this faltering age didst show
Manhood's right image, constant, courteous,
pure,
In silence strong to do and to endure,
'Neath self-suppression veiling inner glow, --

Justice at one with gentleness :--The throe
Of lightning-death found thee, if any, fit,--
Secure in faith,--to bare thy breast to it :--
Ah ! thine the joy, beloved !--ours the woe !

- For thou hast ta'en thine innocence on high,
The child-simplicity of thy stainless years ;
And on thy brows we see the diadem

Of those who walk with Christ in purity,
Fair souls, and wept, like thee, with lifelong tears,
Sword-slain in Ephrataean Bethlehem.

V

SAN CARLO BORROMEO AT ARONA

A TROUBLED image the great Statue threw
   Down on the waters blue,
Where round the lake gray watchful mountains go,
   Frowning beneath the clouds,
And angry summits of eternal snow.

There those who from Arona take their way
   To Belgirate's bay,
Dark o'er the long sweet slopes of vernal green
   Behold that Image set,
High witness how th' unseen transcends the seen.

She too, the Blessèd one, whose golden smile
   Lights up Arona's aisle,
Repeats the message, brought her from above,
   In thrice-inspired art,
And that pure master-piece of tender love.[1]

—But round the green hill, and the height, where he,
   Teaching mankind to see
Their one true God, stands silent evermore,
   The full-voiced nightingale
Thrills the same eloquent song he sang of yore.

[1] See Note

So, Mother !- when thy feet, from earthly tread
  Long sever'd, here were led,
In his due time of joy he sang :   And I
  See the same scene as thou,
With eyes not dimm'd by tears alone,—and sigh :

Foreseeing that inevitable gloom
  Which wraps the nearing tomb ;
Whilst thou, great Saint, above me calm dost stand,
  Urging the way to God,
With that mute eloquence, and imploring hand.

  Ah Saint, and Mother ! Saints together, now
  Ye wait the sign to bow
Before the throne, in final, fullest peace ;
  And cry on those ye love,
Captives of earth, to share the great release.

Baveno; 24 May, 1885

VI

THE LAMENT OF ARGATHELIA [1]

24-25 MAY, 1878

DALRIADA, the dew on thy mountain-tops high
Weeps in silence the night, for thy mistress
must die :
Dark shrouds o'er the summit of Cruachan draw,
And a shuddering flits on the face of Loch Awe.

Over Cowal are voices of terror and grief,
The chiefs of Ergadia lamenting their chief,
Where the sons of Earca and Arthur and Lorne,
Dunolly, and Colin, and Somarled mourn.

Stern souls, who have pass'd to the passionless shore
From the bloodshed and harsh battle-music of yore :
Yet amid the red rapine and whirlwind of life,
Knew the magic and sweetness of daughter and wife.

O well should all hearts on the mountain-side moan !
Though 'tis not for a child of Diarmid they groan,
But for her who in girlhood and graciousness came
To be one with the high-hearted lord of their name.

[1] See Note

As rosebud with rose in the woodland we view,
The bride by her mother in loveliness grew :—
Now, beneath other skies, Love His children has ta'en
Where the roses of God bloom together again.

Dalriada, the mountain-voice lift for the dead !
From thy valleys her sunshine and sweetness are fled :
Bless'd by the eye when it saw her ; and more
By the Master unseen Whose true image she bore.

As the burn to the haugh carries life and increase,
Her feet on the mountains were beauty and peace :
Lips gracious with love ; and around the fair head
The glory of utter unselfishness shed.

O ! the dearest and nearest her praises should tell,
If the tongue could but speak what the heart knows
    too well ;
For she whom the sons of Diarmid deplore
Between beauty and goodness was something yet more !

She is lost to our eyes, but her footsteps are bright
On the path leading upward to light beyond light :
And long will the vision of all she was here
To dark Argathelia's clansmen be dear.

The sky weeps in silence on moorside and brae
For the soul that has pass'd since the passing of day : –
And to-morrow, as dew when the wind hurries o'er,
Dalriada shall seek her, and find her no more.

VII

CHISLEHURST

June, 1879

Purpureos spargam flores. . . .

L ONE Empress, childless widow, whose sad
heart
Knows its own bitterness—and hardly knows—
Death breaking on thee with redoubled blows,
    And soul-benumbing smart ;

    Alone between two memories of past hours ;—
Man has no word for pangs like thine !—yet we
For child and sire take up the dirge, to thee
    Bringing our tears for flowers.

    For he to France gave wealth, with peace, of yore,
And glory, till success and years unnerved
His soul, and from the wiser self he swerved ;
    And flattering friends, the sore

    Which cankers single rule, and that first blot—
A crown by violence compass'd—work'd their will,
And Nemesis on the fatal frontier-hill
    Changed in one hour his lot,

Empire for exile :—and his head he bow'd
With no unmanly grief : while Party hate
Fanatic, o'er his final wreck elate,
    And the foul city-crowd

Spat forth the venom of its seething scum
On the crush'd, broken-hearted chieftain : All
He wrought for France forgotten in his fall !
    —France, of the days to come

Heedless : the shameful cloud with nightly glare
Hung bloodred o'er her streets ; the rebel bands
Kindling death's pile with matricidal hands
    'Gainst their own city fair.

Land of light memories ! enterprises light !
Success alone constrains thy pride to bow !
Ungrateful France ! thine idols crowning now,
    Now burning, in thy spite !

O yet, this day, fair France ! while she apart,
The widow-mother, sits in tearless woe,
Thy better self, thy nobler nature show,
    Thy generous ancient heart !

This hope was hers, this only hope ! —And now !
Past Itelezi, on Edutu's plain,
The wasted life-blood waits the winter's rain,
    Earth's natural tears : But thou,

Seized by the joy of war, and fame in view
With all her sweetness, torrent-like didst go,
Making thy breast the target for our foe
  Where the fell assegai flew.

Marcellus of thy race, untimely fled !
Loyal to France and God ;—too young—too brave !
Whilst we—vain gift !—with violets crown the grave
  Of the loved, honour'd dead.

VIII

IN MEMORY OF CHARLES WELLS AND JOSEPH SEVERN, DYING IN 1879

FRIENDS of young Keats ! Names ne'er to be
forgot,
  While his,—Theocritus of our isle, and more,-
  Is great among our great ones,- -we deplore
Not that, in one sad sunless year, the lot

Of Atropos calls ye to the better spot
  Where Virtue triumphs, and the strife is o'er ;
  But that, with you, the living link that bore
Our souls across the years to him, is not.

Friends of young Keats !—If, on earth's hamper'd
stage,
  Ye kept not all the promise of your prime,
  Yet on each forehead fell the happy ray

Of genius : and we watch'd your honour'd age
  As of those blest ones, who, in earlier time,
  Walk'd with Immortals on life's common way.

IX

PÈRE LA CHAISE

THE field of death at Paris,
  You might think it a fold from afar ;
Like flocks the white tombs scatter'd
  That green enclosure star.

There statesman, financier and poet,
  Love, glory, ambition and guile,
Are laid 'neath their pompous inscriptions,
  And the stranger says ' Who ? ' with a smile.

And some more proudly mock-modest
  Rest under their names alone ;
And all they will soon inherit
  Is but the name and the stone.

There the passionate heart of de Musset
  Sleeps itself tranquil and pure ;
There Béranger, Heine, Bellini,
  Lie 'mid the brilliant obscure ;

He, whose melody echoes the music
  Of the old Sicilian shore ;
And they—in their lifetime too famous
  To be famous for evermore.

But from the white mausolea
  The eye turns wearily soon,
Drawn by the dark fascination
  Of the dreary *Fosse Commune.*

Had these no story of passion ?
  Had these no passion for fame,
No deeds for remembrance or glory,
  Who lie without hillock or name ?

They shovel them in by fifties,
  And bid them lie down with a grin,
Who could not buy a ' concession '—
  Sons of starvation and sin !

Here at last, by Mortality's favour,
  Fraternal and equal they lie :
And the child in vain seeks the mother
  With its cross to crown her, and die.

In this best of worlds, O my brothers,
  Is surely something amiss !
Songs of advance and culture,
  Is your ultimate triumph this ?

Is the soul's heart-hunger abolish'd,
  While agnostics their litany cry,
Or Science says, ' matter to matter,'
  With a smile that lurks in a sigh ? —

The homage and incense of Paris
 On the famous and wealthy are shed ;
But love and sorrow are kneeling
 O'er the undistinguish'd dead ;

And the orphan sobs and wanders
 O'er the dust that will hide it soon
From the wolfish strife for existence.
 In the dreary *Fosse Commune.*

X

AN INVOCATION

COME, Love, as in the golden days
  When I was child and thou wast king ;
Come, poet-wreathed with Lesbian bays,
  And touch each common thing
To heaven by the waving of thy wing.

And crown the crimson wine of life
  With roses of celestial birth,
And bid the banquet-hall be rife
  With strains unheard on earth,
And sadness sweeter than the songs of mirth.

XI

AN ASPIRATION

I T is no fault of the loved one,
  If I cannot discover
Whether my heart be worthy
  To be the heart of her lover.
It is no blot on her beauty
  That makes me wonder and waver,
If to fly the might of her magic,
  Or ask the seal of her favour.

Who could so look onward and upward
  In the faith of his own heart-merits,
When she, young star of the maidens,
  By birth a kingdom inherits?
O Love, who o'er earth and heaven
  Art more than king, O! before her
Bow down, proud Love, in thy glory
  While in thee I kneel and adore her!

O star-drop of liquid silver
  That quivers and flames in the zenith!
Say, what is this entrancement,
  Or what this misery meaneth?

The sapphire spaces about thee
  With the light of thy looks thou palest :
What art thou in thine own heaven,
  If here thou so prevailest ?

Must the spaces that part us
  Still spread darker and wider ?
Can she stoop from her splendour.
  Stoop, and set me beside her ?
Can I climb to her beauty,
  My star with glory above her ?
Or is she too high in heaven
  For me to take her and love her ?

XII

A PAUSE BEFORE BATTLE [1]

21 October, 1805

IN the dreadful calm, before
Thunder-peals of battle roar ;
While each moment, as they go,
Wafts them nearer to the foe ;
While, ere rival courage bleeds,
Life with Death yet intercedes ;—
Kneeling by the bed that ne'er
Thee in life again shall bear,
As they kneel who love and fear,
Admiral, what dost thou here ?

Clear across the brine he sees
Surrey hills, and Merton trees,
Where the fresh autumnal light
Gently gilds a cottage white,
Wall'd with jessamine and rose,
Vision of the heart's repose !
There the Lady of his love
Nestles with the nestling dove ;
There, on baby fitful feet,
Strays the little daughter sweet.

[1] See Note

Darling ! o'er whose sleeping head
His last prayers that night were shed,
Quitting one he loved too well,
With love's pang ineffable.
—Loved not wisely, could he know
How o'er those the years would go,
Desolate and drear, whom he
Left to us, his legacy,
Bitterer tears than tears of war
Had been pour'd for Trafalgar !

Now for these again he pray'd,
Kneeling while the fight delay'd :—
Once more o'er that English home
Saw the sunbeams go and come ;
Saw the garden-child at play
Call'd by Emma's knee to pray ;
O'er the thought once more he smiled,
Lion-soul'd heroic child !
Then his place in calmness takes,
While the battle-thunder breaks.

XIII

THE LOST 'EURYDICE'

24 March, 1878

The mother of a young Officer seen at the helm when the frigate capsized, was waiting his return at Southsea.

'LADY, she is round the Needles: now Saint
   Catherine's Cape they sight:
Now her head is set north-eastward; 'fore the beam
   the Foreland light.

'Look, we see the light from Southsea,'— and beyond
   the fancy goes,
Where e'en now the fated keel is gliding under dark
   Dunnose:

Swanlike gliding, as some cloud that, dark below, the
   storm-wind's hue,
Towers into silver summits, sailing o'er the tranquil
   blue.

O the change!—and in one hour!—when, swanlike,
   on the harbour's breast,
Plumage furl'd and voyage over, safe the gallant ship
   will rest!

—All the movement of the haven spread beneath her
    eyes in vain,
At a window watch'd the Lady, gazing o'er the sunlit
    main ;

Thinking, from the Foreland light-ship they perchance
    e'en now might see,
See the noble ship,   My Ship !—for brings she not my
    boy to me ?

Drifted from the waves the splendour ; from the sky
    died out the blue :
Yet the Lady saw not ; deep beyond herself her sight
    withdrew.

Sunshine glow'd within her bosom ; happy music in
    her ears ;
Love in glory painting all the beauty of his youthful
    years.

Heart 'twixt brave and tender balanced ; manly child,
    and childlike youth :
Bright as heaven, as ocean open ; true to true love,
    true to truth.

' Fit for earth, and. fit for heav'n,' she thinks, ' what-
    e'er his destined lot ; '
—He is there already, Mother ! Mother !—and thou
    know'st it not !

Thunderbolts of icy storm-wind in its panting bosom
    piled,
Sudden, towering angry-black, a cloudy wall climbs
    wide and wild.

Like a squadron at the signal, forth the mad tornado
    flies,
Robed in blinding folds of snow, together mixing seas
    and skies.

—From the window turn, Lady ! toward the light-ship
    look no more ;
Happy that thou canst not see the darkening headland,
    surf-white shore.

Thirty minutes since they watch'd her ;—stately vision,
    jocund crew :—
All beyond from outward witness hidden, lost to
    mortal view.

Voice was none, nor cry of terror ;—as when snow-
    drifts whelm the dell,
Smitten, slain, at once, and buried, where the mad
    tornado fell.

Right upon her side she dipp'd, then turn'd and went
    within the main :
Only at her helm, the last, the gallant boy was seen ;
    —in vain !

—Weep not for thy children, England! though the
    wild waves hold their prey :—
England owns a thousand thousand, loyal to the death
    as they.

Ah ! the sun once more, uncaring, glitters o'er the
    hapless dead,
Golden shafts through twilight emerald piercing to
    their oozy bed.

There, ring'd round with foam-fleck'd waters, flapping
    sails and shatter'd poles
Lift themselves, a desolate beacon, o'er three hundred
    English souls.

There the sun may blaze uncaring, there the ripples
    kiss and play,
Chalk-bright cliffs and grassy headland smiling to
    the smiling bay.

But within the Lady's soul the music and the glow are
    gone ;—
This alone is left to cheer thee, Mother ! Mother !—
    this alone :

Though the heart's desire on earth thy longing eyes
    ne'er meet again,
True to God and England, at the helm, thou seest
    him ;— not in vain !

XIV

THE SUN-DIAL

I LOOK on the happy children,
  And they bid me join their play
By the sun-dial in the garden,
The sun-dial old and gray.

They smile as they watch the shadow
With stealthy resistless pace ;
But they read not the lesson, the dear ones,
Writ on the dial's face.

For you, my children, it numbers
No hours save hours serene ;
No fears for a hidden future,
No pang for the dread ' has been.'

The vision of wasted chances,
Of faces we would not forget
Yet prized not enough when with us,
The deep, unavailing regret :

The years in their torrent swiftness
That shriek as seaward they go . . .
—What know they of this, the children ?
Ah, better they should not know !

They smile and watch by the dial,
Till darkness hurries them hence :
And their souls are bathed in slumber
With the sunshine of innocence.

But I stand and watch them sleeping,
And over their faces go
Flushes and smiles and sweetness,
And breathing even and low.

I muse on the thousand perils
That hang o'er each golden head ;
And I know that my treasures tremble
Like dew on the gossamer-thread.

O Life, what art thou that holdest
What is more than life to thee
By the tenure of thine own hours,
Thine own fragility ?

And each breath is a sigh, that nearer
Brings the long farewell to me :
O were Life not life for ever,
Better life should not be !

XV

TO A CHILD

THE soft blue fire within thine eyes,
    The blush-rose of the rounded cheek,
The curve of the caressing lips
    Moulded to motions meek,—
    All are too fugitive !
These cannot live, my little one !
    These cannot live.

The golden glances in thy hair,
    The grief-unfretted forehead fine,
The gracious harmony of form
    Marr'd by no coarser line ;—
    All are too fugitive !
These cannot live, my little one !
    These cannot live.

As the full birdweed-bloom in June,
    Where purple stain'd on purple lies,
The masterpiece of Flora, one
    One short day burns, and dies,—
    All are too fugitive !
These cannot live, my little one !
    These cannot live.

But the clear message of the eyes
When truth in silence speaks and glows ;
The candour of the faithful lips
　Now rosier than the rose—
　The rose is fugitive—
But these will live, my little one !
　But these will live.

But the mind's inner grace, the form
That 'neath this outward hidden lies ;
More beautiful than beauty's self
　Beneath its dear disguise :—
　These are not fugitive !
These gifts will live, my little one !
　But these will live.

The radiance of the open soul
Pure from all touch of self and ill,
The heart at unison with the head,
　The gracious woman's will :-
　These are not fugitive ;
These, these, will live, my little one !
　These ever live.

September, 1873

XVI

PORTRAIT OF A CHILD OF SEVEN

FAIR Temple ! by some Architect above
  With all-foreknowing power in secret plann'd,
While Grace and Graciousness on either hand,
  And Innocence with Love

Stood by, and shaped each curve to Beauty's line,
With flower-soft touch, more pure than Phidian skill
Or Flaxman's—till the marble miracle
  Shone fair and full and fine,

And breathed and warm'd with life ; like mountain-
    snows
A: dawn, or as beneath Pygmalion's hand
The Parian maid confess'd the soul's command,
  And whiteness flush'd to rose.

—I gaze, and in this living temple know
My seven-years' treasure ; and the soul looks straight
From those bright windows, and the rosy gate
  Smiles in Love's perfect bow.

Fair shrine !—yet of a fairer far within
Thou art but outward mask and symbol weak,
As the sun's shadow, moonlight ;—and we seek
  The soul beneath the skin,

Veil'd and incarnated in lineament,
Limb, footstep, finger, gesture, voice, caress ;
And e'en to silken hair, to childly dress,
  By loving fancy lent.

Fair soul ! young hidden inmate ! yet no less
Seen in the crystal clear intelligence,
The deep-heart love, the meditative sense,
  The pure unselfishness ;

While (Reynolds in each line), by me she stands
With violet steadfast eyes, and pensive smile
Of absolute faith, and lays on mine the while
  Her soft caressing hands :--

Till now one perfect whole of heavenly art,
Inward and outward, in the child I trace ;
Harmonious as some type of Raphael grace,
  Or strain of sweet Mozart.

21 March, 1879

XVII

L'IMPRÉVU

PORTH GWYN, DINLLEYN

DEAR child, methought, how often have we turn'd
    The page where art sets forth a scene like
this, –
The rocks, the cove, the green green waves that kiss
Their pebbled beach,––and for the spot have yearn'd !

—Wilful, why would'st not come ?—Here at my feet
The rustling of the ever-restless sea
Round each dark shatter'd rock runs foamingly
With quick inrush of flood, and quick retreat :

Yet not this soft-flush'd dome of Autumn sky,
    Those golden sands that clasp the Shining Bay,
      And smile their welcome to that nearing tide

The heart's desire can wholly satisfy,—
    All Nature's beauty here, and thou away !
      —A touch—a kiss :—and she was at my side.

12 September, 1883

XVIII

IN MEMORIAM

AS I wander o'er hillside and meadow
I think of the children three ;
I hear the pure blithe voices,
The fair fair faces I see.

Frank, blue-eyed, sturdy, and smiling ;
Gwenllian rounded and fine ;
And the lips of the little eldest
Than coral more coralline.

And the glory of youth and gladness
Is in all that they do and say,
And they walk without past or future
In the light of an endless to-day.

But I from the past look onward
To a future hidden from you ;
And I trace this image of childhood
For the eyes of hereafter to view :

That when mine are fallen to darkness,
They may rest on the picture awhile,
With a smile, my darlings no longer !
That is not altogether a smile.

XIX

THE HAPPY VALLEY

IN the heart of the long bare uplands
   It lies like a river of green ;
And the trees each slope descending
Leave a flowery sward between :—

A flowery path for the children,
With the oak and the thorn on high ;
Coverts to tempt the boldest,
And shelter-spots for the shy.

Come, Love, to the happy valley
Where the turf slopes smooth and dry :
At our feet the laughing children ;
Above, the laughing sky.

Life has no hour more golden
Than thus on the grassy slope :
While we blend the age of reason
With the brighter age of hope.

For Childhood is of the valley,
Haven'd from tempest and heat ;
With flowers beyond its grasping,
And flowers beneath its feet ;

Mid-age has the long bare uplands,
Bare to the heat and the rain :—
Come, Love, to the happy valley,
Children with children again.

XX

CHILDREN'S LAMENT FOR BABY

DEAR little Baby day by day
    We watch'd as on the bed it lay ;
And oft its eyes it open'd wide, ·
And smiled to see us at its side :—
The clothes are on the empty bed ;
But where is little baby fled ?

Its limbs were growing long and fine,
Its hands put out to clasp and twine ;
The lips began to coo and call ;
It sat upright and wish'd to crawl ;
And brighter daily round its head
The golden hair like sunrise spread.

When first within the cot it lay,
We ask'd if it had come to stay ;
And scream'd for joy to hear them tell
'Twas sent from God with us to dwell,
And play about till it was grown,
And be our very very own.

And when its eyes were sunk and dim,
And wasting seized each tiny limb,
We nursed it on our knees all day,
And begg'd it not to go away :
It moved its head and faintly cried,
And then lay still and sigh'd and sigh'd.

And now we cry and look in vain,
And cannot see it here again :—
The cot is white and still and bare,
But baby smiles and sings elsewhere ;
Among God's Angels bright and dear :
Yet not more Angel there than here.

XXI

VERE NOVO

SWEET primrose-time ! When thou art here
    I go by grassy ledges
Of long lane-side, and pasture-mead,
    And moss-entangled hedges :

And all around her army gay
    The primrose weather musters,
In single knots, and scatter'd files,
    And constellated clusters.

And golden-headed children go
    Among the golden blossoms,
And harvest a whole meadow's wealth,
    Heap'd in their dainty bosoms.

Ah ! Play your play, sweet little ones,
    While life is gladness only :
Nor ask an equal mirth from hearts
    Which, e'en with you, are lonely.

God to His flowers His flowers gives,
    Pure happiness uncloying ;
Whilst they, whose primrose-time is past,
    Enjoy in your enjoying.

XXII

A LATE SPRING

The Marriage of Zephyrus and Chloris [1]

LATE Zephyr, thou this month and more art
    dallying
  In some sweet western cave,
  Atlantis, or Ogygia, where the wave
Laps thee in sleep, or some white Goddess-form
    Holds back thy sallying.

Within the gracious haunts of early flowering
  Idly the children seek
  Thy children,—primrose, speedwell, hyacinth
    meek ;
While in this March-May breeze the windflower-stars
    Shine faint and cowering.

The violet only comes, the true-heart's favourite,—
  And on the trees meanwhile,
  Chloris, thy bride, looks vainly for a smile,
A breath, excusing thy delay ; and thou
    Hast nought to say for it.

[1] See Note

But she, forgetful of the days of flowering,
  Sits in the forest gray,
  And all her buds blush reddening at thy stay,
And cannot weave their rose-wreaths for the bride,
  Or green embowering.

What ails thee, Zephyr, while the blackbird clamor-
  ous
  Calls thee to Chloris' side,
  Mocking thy chilling absence from the bride ;
While the sad silent nightingale holds back
  His welcome amorous ?

Come, Zephyr, come ! the heavens one moment
  favouring,
  Invite thee from the west ;
  Fair Chloris woos thee to her genial breast ;
Spring waits the bridal, sick of this delay,
  And long, long wavering.

May, 1879

XXIII

NATURAE REPARATRICI

SWEET fleckless sky, May heralding
　　All Summer's joys together,
Vine-wreath, rose, myrtle, nightingale,
And youth's unclouded weather :

Thy sunshine is my gloom : I mourn
　　Young Hope, aims idly cherish'd ;
The faces seen no more on earth,
　　The priceless years, the perish'd.

Yet Nature holds a gracious hand,
　　Her ancient way pursuing ;
And spreads the charms we loved of old,
　　To aid the heart's renewing.

Here her long crests of sky-ward crag
　　Allure the unresting swallows ;
Here still the dove's low love-note floats
　　Above her leafy hollows.

Here its calm strength her hillside rears
From heaving slopes of clover ;
Here still the pewit pipes and flits
Within his furzy cover.

Here hums the wild-bee in the thyme,
Here glows the royal heather ;
And youth comes back upon the breeze,
And youth's unclouded weather.

XXIV

A HALCYON DAY IN SUMMER

THOUGH thy song-tribute ne'er has fail'd, O Sea !
  Since that Aeolian Master set thy soul
  To music in his long hexameter roll,
One gift, in these changed years, I bring to thee : -

For thou to-day hast veil'd thy majesty
  'Neath this smooth shining floor of purpled green,
  Pattern'd with white waves o'er the gloom unseen
Where gray Leviathan circles fast and free :—

On such a day might Galataea fair
  Flaunt her fleet dolphins o'er the buoyant plain,
    While Zephyrs dipt and vaulted through the sky :

- Now one lone bird, wheeling, her hungry prayer
  Screams forth, responsive to the low refrain
    Of thy sweet, sad, eternal litany.

LYME, *September*, 1888

XXV

A DORSET VALLEY

Between Monkton Wyld and Reed's Barn, Lyme

IT is no cemented mile-path,
  Of Rome's imperial day,
That drives over down and valley—
  Right onward its ruthless way :

Nor in years of the mine and the furnace
  Was it laid by a later hand,
To be one of the veins of iron
  Which bear the pulse of the land :—

But the path that I show you, children,
  Has an older way of its own,
And took its sweet steps through the valley
  Ere Roman and Saxon were known.

It winds like a grassy streamlet
  'Twixt hollies and hazels old,
And the palms of silvery velvet,
  Where the willow-wren twinkles in gold.

Where the wayside slopes are embosom'd
  In gorse and the feathery brake ;
Where the round root-stems of the beeches
  Coil like a gray old snake :

Where the sky is pierced with the arrows
  Of the sweet shrill linnet aloft,
And red robin and black bird answer
  With mellower song from the croft ;

And the cottages peep in their whiteness
  'Mid the holts of the valley wild,
And shine as the smile that lightens
  The face of a pensive child ;

And little ones stand in the doorway
  With their handfuls of cowslip gold,
While the smoke goes white from the hearthstone,
  As it went in the days of old :—

And we smile as we see the children
  Smile in their valley green ;
Our relic spared from Old England ;
  Our own dear Dorset scene.

XXVI

BETWEEN NIGHT AND MORNING

IN SOUTH-WESTERN ENGLAND

STILL, still,—so still that you might carve,
  Like marble in the bed,
Vast blocks of solid silence, from
  The night around us spread :
Till stealthy-glimmering dawn with gray
  Dilutes the ebon dark,
And tuning for the sky his song,
  Awakes the woodland lark.

Thou Dawn that silent flood'st the vale,
  Wilt flood the vale with song,
While tremulous wing and open'd beak
  In their green nurseries throng.
With those who chaunt His praise, and float
  Through Heaven their order'd way,
God's little ones of hedge and holt
  Their angel-service pay.

Now o'er the bay a second sea
  Of liquid amber swims :
Each grove now to the gracious light
  Breaks forth in thankful hymns :
With jocund cry the blackbird trim
  Leaps on the dewy lawn :—
O snow-soft silence of the night !
  O music of the dawn !

XXVII

A SUMMER SUNSET

IN SOUTH-WESTERN DORSET

THIS hour is given to peace :—
The downward-slanting sunbeams graze the vale
Where Even breathes her stealthy gathering gray ;
 And o'er white stubble-plots, the sheaves
Like walls of gold put forth their ripe array.

 Upon the green slope sward
The hedgerow elms lie pencill'd by the sun
In greener greenness : and, athwart the sky,
 Dotted like airy dust, the rooks
Oar themselves homeward with a distant cry.

 And the whole vale beneath,
To Castle Lammas' violet-bosom'd height,
With all its wealth outspread of harvest hopes,
 Half green, half russet gold, runs up
As a fair tapestry shaken o'er the slopes.

 It is an utter calm !
The topmost ash-tree sprays have ceased to wave ;
The cushat checks her sweet redoubled moan ;
 And e'en the gray-wall'd cottages
Sleep 'mid their crofts like things of Nature's own

I hear the shepherd's call ;
The white specks gather to the crowding fold,
Their lowly palace of unvex'd repose :
   While o'er the chambers of the sun
Float filmy fleeces of empurpled rose.

   And now the silent moon
Lifts her pale shield above a glassy sea,
And from the highest cloud the sunbeams cease :
   And, tranced in Nature's holy hour,
The time-sick heart renews its ancient peace.

   —Then in the soul we know
The presence of our dear ones : Love binds up
The sore of life, and pours himself in balm :
   While e'en the memories of the dead
Glide painless through the breast in star-like calm.

XXVIII

AUTUMN

WITH downcast eyes and footfall mild,
      And close-drawn robe of lucid haze,
The rose-red Summer's russet child
      O'er field and forest Autumn strays :
On lawn and mead at rising day
Tempers the green with pearly gray ;
And 'neath the burning beech throws round
A golden carpet on the ground.

And oft a look of long regret
      Her eyes to Summer's glory throw :
Delaying oft the brand to set
      That strips the blossom from the bough :
And where in some low shelter'd vale
The last sweet August hues prevail,
Her eager frosts she will repress,
And spare the lingering loveliness.

And for her searing hours of night
      And narrow'd spaces of her day,
By sudden smiles of mellow light
      And azure gleams she strives to pay ;

With cluster'd coral tempts the bird
To livelier song than Summer heard,
Till the loud flutings of his strain
Cheat him almost to Spring again.

Yet, in her own despite, her sway
  Leads down the year to gloom and cold,
And all the green delight of May
  Her touch transmutes to barren gold :
As Age, that crowns with wealth our years,
Dries the sweet spring of human tears,
And while to pride of state we press,
Kills the soul's inner fruitfulness.

Ah ! whilst her stealthy hands unbare
  The naked trellis of the groves,
Black Winter laughs within his lair,
  And revels in the wreck he loves :
And knows his hour will soon be here
To cast his shroud upon the year,
And o'er the white hill-side and vale
To ride and ravage on the gale.

And though beneath the snow-mass'd slope
  The harvests of the future lie,
No hue of life, no hint of hope:
  Lights the dead earth and spectral sky :

And all the promise of the Spring
Is like a hidden far-off thing ;
A dream too tender, faint, and sweet,
For mortal eyes again to meet.

No ! The dear hopes that grow more dear
   With sterner self-restraint we quell ;
And what lies hid within the year
   We would not, if we could, foretell.
No !- -And if once again we see
The green leaf glorify the tree,
The gray sky glisten into blue,
It will not be the Spring we knew.

XXIX

FROM LUCERNE

IF I could put my love in words,
  Would I pour out to Thee
A sweeter song than any yet
  Was sung by bird on tree :—

Here, where the many-pointed Mount
  That wears the cap on high,[1]
Pale against paler air, builds up
  His snows beneath the sky ;

Or where, above an English sea,
  Our green hills fringe the bay,
The long sweet hours of eve we sit,
  Till golden fades to gray.

—But as who, at some shrine long-sought,
  Would speak, but cannot dare,
So much the Presence overawes
  The pilgrim and the prayer ;

So am I mute : Yet, to the soul
  Can that dumb silence tell
In words beyond art's choicest art,
  How well I love,— how well !

May, 1885

[1] See Note

XXX

AN AUTUMN SONG

TO EUGENIA

SUMMER hay and harvest
   Come and gone again :
Ah ! the months are measured
   By the yellow wain !
As the stately cargoes
   Down the valley sway ;
Golden wheat-sheaf mountains,
   Hills of scented hay.

Yearly for her children
   Earth, the Mother, pours
Thus in rick and linhay
   Her sustaining stores :
Heedless if the ploughman
   Reap the seed he sows,
If with grass and leaf-bud
   He o'erlive the snows.

Man she loves ; but loves not
   With a mother's heart ;
'Tis the race that only
   In her care has part.

For the Whole providing.
  Deaf to each one's fate,
She our tears and laughter
  Eyes with smile sedate.

—Down a twilight ocean
  Men like swimmers go ;
Some sweet face beside them,
  Some few voices know.
Faint and firm the Pole star
  Beaconing overhead,
O'er the heaving billows
  Draws a silver thread.

Who knows when his nearest
  'Neath the flood shall go ?
Who, when Death may call him
  From the night below ?—
—Shall we see the spring-time,
  Hear the bird again ?
Ask no more, when autumn
  Brings the harvest wain !

Swaying down the hillside,
  On the hedge it weaves
Lines of golden wheat-straw
  That outlast the leaves :
  Shall we see the spring-time
  Bud and burst again ?—
Ask no more, Eugenia !
  Ask no more in vain !

XXXI

A VISION OF LIFE

DAYS come and days go by,
    Gliding so fast that one
Into another almost seems to run,
And Thursday dawns ere Wednesday is nigh :
One precious leaf each plucking from the tree
    Of life allotted me.

Through the thinn'd boughs atop
    Looks in the naked blue ;
The flowers all fall'n, and scanty fruit in view,
Sweet-ripe to pull, or set for future crop ;
And at the root the hidden worm I know
    Mining to lay it low.

Ah tree, that once in youth,
    When hope was green and high,
Dreamt its large leafy head would touch the sky,
Its roots all matted round the central truth !
How poor, by that vast visionary tree,
    Looks the small shrub I see !

Not rooted in pure truth
But in some shifting soil,
Where error and appearance mock our toil,
Till freezing Age seals the bold eyes of Youth,
Saying, ' *Look here! for all thy force and glow,*
Thou canst no farther go.'

Yet, though the leaves may fall,
The life-sap is not shrunk,
But gathers strength deep in the knotted trunk,
And, losing part, has more than having all ;
Condensed within itself to meet the stress
Of age, with cheerfulness.

And for the dreams of youth
Come larger aims, that bear
Elsewhere their fruit, their crown expect elsewhere,
In amaranth meadows of immortal truth,
Where the sun sets not all our night below
O'er flowers of golden glow :

Unfading leaves, and eyes
Wiped from all human tears ;
Soft gliding of the years that are not years,
Eternal spaces : -not like those our sighs
Note as they pass, while, fast as bubbles fly,
Days come and days go by.

XXXII

BETWEEN GRAVE AND CRADLE

SHE will not come again, or bless thy bed,
   Fair lamb asleep, softer than thy soft nest ;
Or count the heavings of a grandchild's breast,
Kissing the pure fresh lips rose-garlanded,
    Life's open gates :- Ah vain, ah vain ;
      She will not come again.

Unseen by her thy face, warm nestled Dove,
   Snatch'd ere she knew the fruitful hours to be,
   Her own child's blessedness fulfill'd in thee,
This waxen miniature, this roseblush Love :
    Here, Angel Mother, here !—Ah vain—
      She will not come again.

Thou smil'st on me : thy baby grasp repays
   The touch of mine : I see her in thy face :
   Her heart informs the lastling of her race :
I hear the fairy feet of jocund days,
    The dear remember'd voice : Ah vain ;
      She will not come again.

Sweet smiler ! so ! 'tis blithe Love foots the stair,
  A mother's carol cry beyond the door :—
  O she would smile to hear, who smiles no more,
And bid me wipe the fond tears of despair
    And joy where all is joy :—Ah vain—
      She will not come again.

XXXIII

ELEGY ON THE DEPARTED

E se non piangi, di che pianger suoli?

O FIELD of God, with grassy waves
   Spread as a summer sea,
What peace is o'er thine inmates pour'd :
   Oh that 'twere so with me !

There 'neath the holy Cross the sods
   Her soul's fair vesture hold ;
The ransom'd spirit borne meanwhile
   To Jesus' happy fold.

But to my side, by night, by day,
   The mortal arrow cleaves :
Earth's cup of innocent delight
   A wormwood savour leaves.

I shun the seat whence oft we watch'd
   The sunset rose the sky :
All Nature's charm before me flits
   As o'er a dead man's eye.

In each fair spot a memory hid
   The heart with torture scars :
The hills by those dear eyes last seen
   I see through blinding tears.

Ah sweet Spring days by lamb-starr'd lea,
 Fresh feathery grove, and glen ;
All earth with three-fold beauty blest,—
 For thou with me wert then !

Or where 'neath some tall cliff the sea
 Her peacock bosom raised,
And smiled a bluer, tenderer smile
 As by thy side I gazed !

Now o'er the lightsome skies a pall
 Of rayless gray has come,
For with her going hence is gone
 The sunshine of the home.

I dread the door where those soft steps
 Have pass'd, and pass'd away :
The bedside where my Saint in Heaven
 Bow'd low for Heaven to pray.

— O fond faint eyes that turn'd to me
 In that last, bitterest woe !
O Love, Love, Love, my Love, my own,
 How could'st thou leave me so ?

Still o'er the lawn the star-eyed sky
 Lets fall her silver tears :
The rose that knew thy tending hand,
 Her heedless beauty rears :

They reck not, they, that thou art gone,
  Nor how earth's minutes run
While thy dear face withdrawing fades
  As mist in morning sun.

O deeper than the deepest pang
  The form from memory chased ;
Love's empty vase with ashes fill'd,
  The wound by Time effaced !

Sad years that dim the dear, dear face
  As round your circles sweep !
Dearest, did I not weep thee now,
  How should I ever weep?

Still to my side by night, by day,
  The mortal arrow clings :
The fair fresh breeze of dawn may waft
  No comfort on her wings :

The soft security of sleep,
  The blessings of the night,
These sorrow-streaming eyes in vain
  In vain to rest invite.

O Heaven on which my soul I cast
  With all the force of faith,
From thy pure crystal depths reveal
  That holy Spirit-Wraith !

Mother ! be with me as thou wert—
   Or if the heavenly place
Have wrought the change, the aureoled head,
   Sure I shall know thy face !

The hand that almost o'er my brow
   Breathed in its soft caress ;
The peace on the fair forehead sign'd,
   The step, the very dress :—

Smile as when once the tender eyes
   Upon thy baby smiled ;
On that pure bosom let me rest,
   And be thy child, thy child !

—Ah, silence in that azure sky,
   And on this grassy field !
And silence on thy lips to me
   By law almighty seal'd !

Not here, not here, but where the Blest
   Their crown of victory win ;
Where the Redeemer and the Life
   Welcomes His faithful in.

   What sudden voice the stillness stirs,
   What low sweet loving cry ?
About her Cross, lo ! where the dove
   Circles and sweeps on high.

O Mother, Mother mine, my soul
   Mounts with the mounting dove :
Almost I seem thy steps to trace
   To Heavens the heaven above !

—Thou first blest sign of peace to man,
   Love's own sweet messenger !
Where my Saint sits, God grant me wings
   To rise and follow her.

1891

AMENOPHIS

14'

THE framework of this story has been taken, with some modifications, from an Egyptian version of the *Exodus*, quoted by Josephus from the native historian Manetho. "After 518 years, as Josephus thinks, had passed since the expulsion of the Hyksôs, a King named Amenophis was seized by the desire of beholding the Gods, a blessedness which he knew had been reached by Horos, one of his ancestors. He spoke of this wish to a son of Paapis, who because he was thought to be wise and to see into futurity was held to share himself in the divine nature. This man showed Amenophis that his wish might be fulfilled, if he would purge the land of lepers and other unclean persons." The rest will be found in Josephus' essay "against Apion," or by the English reader in the paraphrase given by Ewald in his "History of Israel," translated by Mr. R. Martineau. For other materials Herodotus, the earlier Greek poets, and the narrative of "Exodus," have been chiefly used : and the beautiful Ode "To Ligurinus," paraphrased in the third Book, has not been thought inappropriate, as it is clearly one of those which Horace took from lost Hellenic originals.

The main aim of the whole is, however, to set forth briefly, with as much accuracy to fact as the writer (un-versed in Egyptology) could reach, the ideas upon the exist-ence of God, and His relation to man and the world, held by the Egyptian, Greek, and Jewish races during the period when these ideas had not been consciously analysed and clothed in philosophical form. The vastness of the interests concerned in these problems, on which all views of life which recognize anything beyond existence within the bounds of mortality are founded, might seem to render it unnecessary to unite them with a story even of such high human interest as that which belongs to the Israelitish Exodus. But the writer's wish (however imperfect its accomplishment), has been to show, in the guise of a little tale, the inner essence of those early beliefs, named above, historically, and without any attempt to compare or to moralize on them : for which purpose the narrative form of Poetry is better suited than the didactic. And the motive assigned to Amenophis by the historian appears to justify the selection of the story told by Manetho as the groundwork for the thoughts with which it has been here attempted to unite it.

AMENOPHIS

THE SEARCH AFTER GOD

BOOK I

GORGEOUS in pride, and satiate full with bliss,
  Within his halls sate King Amenophis,
The sacrifice just over : for the steam
Yet curl'd round each gay-chequer'd cedar-beam
And roof-recess, from Amoûn's altar high.
Meanwhile the ram was slain, and cautiously
The red-skinn'd priests o'er Amoûn's golden face
The bearded muzzle of the creature place,
And cautiously the form of Horus bring
And set it fronting that ram-facéd thing,
Beating themselves for Horus' sake, that he
So mask'd alone the holy face must see,
And then go down his journey to the west,
And up the skies again, and find no rest.

For so the story runs, that Horus pray'd
Himself to see God face to face, and laid
Such heart into his prayer, that the Most High
Before the hero pass'd disguisedly,
Veiling his glory 'neath a creature's face.

And Horus look'd, and went about his ways :
Though now he sits before him in the skies,
And sees God face to face without disguise.

Amenophis survey'd the annual rite ;
Symbol half-dimm'd through Time's effacing night.
Each priest now put aside his lissom rod,
And knelt before him, and invoked as God.
Then something stirr'd within his vaulted breast,
And prick'd his pride and woke a vague unrest.
He call'd aloud and said
                    ' Before the King
' Life's lordly pageant, all her pleasures, bring ;
' That he may view them all, and judge, and try.'

Then first the train of dancing-maids went by :
Each lustrous bosom, to the mid-waist bared,
Fit pillow for the King's own head prepared ;
Each virgin form suggesting new delight ;
Each suppliant archly for one bridal night.

So they pass'd onwards : and Amenophis sigh'd.
    Then thirty Ethiopians, ebon-dyed,
In golden vessels bore red gold heap'd up.
The gleamy harvest overran the cup,
Waste unregarded.   Next, an equal train
Brought other stores of parti-colour'd grain
In Ethiopia glean'd and Arya far :—
Carbuncles, redder than the warrior star,

Sapphirus, Amethystus, and the light
Of Adamas, that rivals in his might
The sun, when o'er Syéné zenith high :—
Then Emeralds, to take the wearied eye
And bathe it in a bath of greener green
Than sun-smit tarns from Eira's summit seen.
Save 'mong the treasures of earth's garner-floor,
Where, age on age, the gnomes their jewels store,
None e'er were known, or dreamt in poet's dream,
Like those that now on Egypt's master gleam.

So these pass'd onwards : and Amenophis sigh'd.
   Now through the pillar'd corridors and wide
High-lighted hall soft wailings fill'd the space,
And low pulsations moved with even pace,
As though the heart that eased itself in song
Beat 'neath its own voice with a sense of wrong,
Delicate agony ; painful delight, and strong.
Now Maneros' and Lityerses' name
Through the high-sorrowing dulcimers oft came.
And Linus young, who withers in his bloom,
And hides each summer in the ocean-tomb,
The yearly darling of the Syrian maid :—
A tale from Libanus to Nile convey'd.
Like wind-swept wheat at that belovèd word
Smote on each harp runs up a shivering chord ;
And all the voices blend in one long strain,
That circled snake-like round the pillar'd fane :

—Fair O fair beyond all fairness here,
In thine own season to thine own appear :
O Linus young, who wither'st in thy bloom,
Wake, the Spring summons, in thy salt sea tomb ;
The Amathusian calls thee : Linus, come !

As one the bosom of the crowd was moved
Beneath the Linus' song, the lost, the loved :
Eyes large and humid ; bosoms big with sighs,
Long sighs, and love, and voiceless ecstasies.
But with a short and broken laugh, the King
Turn'd in his throne, as one half-wakening
From fever'd sleep, and rose and left the hall :
Stopping his ears when past the sight of all,
And moving fast, and sometime looking round,
To know when safe beyond the reach of sound.

But as he saw that giant temple lie
Behind like one great bank against the sky,
He stay'd his stumbling pace across the sands,
Pressing together, palm on palm, his hands,
And wing'd his sight through the deep vault of blue,
And gazed as if the soul could pierce it through,
Mounting through sphere o'er sphere of lucent air :
And then fell flat, and spoke out his despair.

' O whether Amoûn or Osiris named,
' Or some dread sound as yet by man unframed,

If once to Horus thou didst bend thine ear,
'Amenophis, another suppliant, hear !
'The King of Kings and Lord of Lords below,
' One only boon I beg thee to bestow.
' If thou be He that made the earth and skies,
' To thine own creature come without disguise.
· Long have I blindly groped around thy throne,
' But the sense sees not what the heart has known.
' I strain for thee, I gaze with eager nerves,
'.But my glance backward to my eyeballs curves ;
· To meet thine arms my arms I fling abroad ;
' My arms fold on me, vacant of the God.
' Upon the dark I paint thy secret face,
' But night holds nothing in her hollow space.
' Dost thou not see my tears, not hear my cry ?
' I cannot see nor hear, yet know thee nigh.
' I feel thee in the dust-wreaths of the plain,
' And in the rare, quick drops of sacred rain :
' I seek thee round the corners of the rocks,
' Or on the riverain pasture of the flocks ;
' And thou art there, but art not there for me : —
' Take all the world, all else I yield to thee :
' But I must see the God before I die.'

He spoke.   His own voice was the sole reply.
    Then a small hand went lightly o'er his head
Softening the deep-brown curls : and Anaïs said,
Anaïs the Ionian slave, the most beloved,
    'O King, for great things art thou greatly moved'?

But he : ' I would see God before I die.'

Then Anaïs with low voice resignedly :

'What is it that he says, Amenophis,
'*In this thing only have I set my bliss*
'*To see God ere I die?* Is not he God?
'By what more noble foot is Egypt trod?
'His form as very God's? Is not he Lord,
'Aye, Lord of Lords, the fear'd one, the adored?
'I saw him by the golden Horus stand,
'And he seem'd born for worship and command.
'Ionia's Gods are fairer far than these,
'Nor would I aught dispraise the deities :
'Yet when my trembling eyes first scann'd his face,
'Lordliest and best meseem'd of human race ;
'And me he chose out from all else, and cried
'*Nothing should part us, Anaïs, ere we died.*
'What word is that, *I would see God and die.*'

Then the King's form rose up against the sky.

Meanwhile the sun had sunk, and overhead
E'en as they gazed, and ere the words are said,
The whole sky went at once from blue to red,
Like sapphire furnace-fused to carbuncle.
The rosy radiance over Egypt fell ;
The hills around and sand-plains caught the flood ;
The river ran a burning belt of blood.
Then, North and South, a trembling 'gan to shake
The fiery curtain of the sky, and break

Its crimson foldings : then the blue look'd through,
And all the heaven unflush'd itself anew.
Faint grays and tender azures float afar,
And purple after-glows the horizon bar ;
And lo ! the tremulous silver of the twilight star.

Both gazed in silence on the arching skies,
And turn'd and look'd within each other's eyes.
'—What more would'st grasp, what more, Amenophis ?
' What closer perilous Vision ask than this ?
' Is not His presence in the aether far,
' His eyes and glory in the twilight star ?
' What nearer nearness, man to God, would'st have ' ?
    But he : ' These things are not the thing I crave.
' For I would see him plain before I die :
' Let all the world, and all in it, go by.'

Then with a little tremor in her voice,
    ' O King, in your God can I not rejoice !
' Harsh in their aspect are the Gods of Nile,
' That call men off from love and joy and smile :
' Far other those Ionian maidens love,
' Not alien so from man, so far above.
' O Delian archer, when thou climb'st the sky,
' Enough for me to watch thy car go by ;
' To know that Hypereion's form is there,
' And drink his beauty in the golden air.
' O Cyprian queen, enough to see thy smile
' As the light waves lap in on Lesbos' isle ;

' To breathe thee 'mong the violet beds at dawn,

' To read thy rosy footsteps on the lawn.

' —Was it for this, that I was nursed and bred,

' And train'd fit partner for the royal bed,

' And taught the name of Love, and tasted thine?

' O me, I fear a common fate is mine ;—

' Man holds out love to woman first, and then

' Flies, and she vainly chases him again.

' Another common fate I also prove :

' He loves her for himself, she him for love.

' Art thou so prompt to yield the world and me

' For some high vision that thou ne'er wilt see ?

' Will sight of God be more to thee than this —

' Ah, take it ! ah, refuse me not thy kiss !

' Say, shall I tire thee with my baby words ?

' Bear with me : speech some little aid affords.

' —What was it first, the magic and the power

' That drew me so to thee ? The day, the hour,

' The minute I remember ; and the fear,

' Thou would'st not look, and know how thou wert
    dear.

' I went before thee slowly down the hall,—

' O might I turn and on thy bosom fall !

' Before thy feet I spread the rushes green,

' That thy feet might go where my hands had been :

' I kiss'd the fringéd curtains of the bed,

' And where thy neck would be, and where thy head

' And shook and listen'd and my face conceal'd,

' And yet was ready at a look to yield.

—I tell thee all, by maiden-shame reproved :
' Thou never knew'st before how thou wert loved.
    ' Now as thou wilt, my sovereign, do with me.
' A little while love made me equal thee :
' Now I am nought, and thou the King of men.'

She bow'd her face, and knelt to him again.
Then, where behind the head a little space
Lay white below her dark hair's braided grace.
He kiss'd her, parting with his hand the braid.
And by her hand he led the slender maid,
Smoothing her odorous tresses oft and oft,
While Love came wafted on the perfume soft,
And brought her where the palace, long and vast,
Lay like a hill-side gainst the horizon cast.

But when the night was well advanced, the two
Rose from their couch, and to the casement drew.
Then Anaïs look'd forth on the landscape fair,
And Sirius quivering in the crystal air ;
And said ' I cannot fathom thy desire,
' But feel it smouldering in the heart like fire.
' Then lest it lay thee waste in ashes, take
' Some counsel of the wise this heat to slake.'
    And he : ' O Love, O ever wise and true,
' There is nought else but this for me to do.
' And I have heard Paapis, priest of On,
' Dying, bequeath'd such wisdom to his son.

' That he, if any, can set forth the road
' Which brings a man in presence of the God.
' So be it, then, to-morrow, as thou say'st.'
   With that, he slept his last untroubled rest.
For with the morrow to the palace came
The dark-hair'd sage of more than mortal fame,
Such signs and wonders at his hand were wrought :
Yet to see God his power availéd nought.
And evil counsel gave he to the King.

' O master, much about the Gods men sing,
' That they are great and strong and just and wise :—
' And I should hold them foolish who despise
' Such speech : for they are strong, and just, and
     great :
' Yet are they also jealous and irate.
' All prayers but of the loyal they refuse,
' Who do them service in the mode they choose.
  ' Now in this land where once the Faith was one,
' A monstrous thing and horrible is done.
' For there be some who mock the blesséd Gods,
' And those who minister in their abodes,
' And say that Amoûn, far beyond our ken,
' Dwells not in temples made by hands of men,
' And little cares for sacrifice or priest.
' Also they reck not where the soul deceased
' Passes, or ask if it exist again ;
' For *These things to the God alone pertain.*

'Also to shepherd life and flocks they lean.
' Now, though the men are sordid, poor, and mean,
' Nay, cursed by God's own finger, for the most
' With leprosy are smitten, white as frost,
' Yet do the poorer sort their counsels hear ;
' And so the crowd grows stronger, year by year.
' These therefore, if the God thou would'st behold,
' Drive from the land, Amenophis ; be bold ;
' For on the side of God the war will be.'

Then with a sudden hiss from throat to knee
Amenophis rent his robe, and o'er his head
Flung ashes from the altar-top, and said :
   ' Son of Paapis, now the sign I know
' Seen yesternight : if it be this or no,
· (I will recount it), say ; for thou art wise.
   ' I was in dreams where Rhampsinitus lies,
' And from the chamber of his coffin went
' A downward slope of shining stone, that bent
' Its way to central earth, where Isis great
' In the dim realm of death, Amenthes, sate.
' Like Rhampsinitus, there I diced : yet not
' Like him, for her game gain'd the alternate lot ;
' And when mine fell, a Syrian robed in snow
' Snatch'd all the lucky dice, and foil'd the throw.
' And Isis frown'd and said, *The toil is vain.*
' Then on the tables fell a crimson rain ;
' And as the vision fled, I heard, *The toil is vain.*

'— But now I know the vainness of the toil.
' First will I sweep and cleanse the holy soil
' Of these profane, the scum of Hyksôs' brood,
' Fit leaders of the leprous multitude.
' Then, having purified the land from ill,
' Thou shalt entreat for me Osiris' will,
' That I may know what sacrifices best
' Will bend the God to grant me my behest,
' That I may see his glory, even I.'

' So be it,' the magician made reply :
' But for the men are many, and their creed
' Allures both them who have, and them who need,
' And that their chieftain, nursed up as a boy
' In all our wisdom, now to our annoy
' Ungrateful turns the magic lore he gain'd,
' A royal slave within thy halls maintain'd,
' Best to begin with hallow'd guile, and then
' Smite the base throng, their leaders being slain,
' Defeated in their atheist palmistry.
' For by the skill that Hermés lodged in me
' Here in thy presence will I show them fools,
' And Amoûn only he that is and rules.
' This done, they will be readily thy prey.'
  So spake he, and departed on his way.

BOOK II

AGAIN within the pillar'd hall and high
Amenophis sate and watch'd the hours go by,
Whilst at the throne's foot the long shadow pass'd
From the tall gnomon o'er the pavement cast.
    Meanwhile the leaders of the Syrian throng,
Marvelling and moved at thoughts of threaten'd
        wrong,
Beneath Osarsiph range them in the hall,
Osarsiph, their great chief, and soul of all:

Like one of those gray pillars he stood there,
Firm in himself alone, with quiet air
Doing his office : somewhat scant in phrase
And mild of aspect : but his mouth betrays
Throughness that cannot falter ; and his eye
On some far vision dwells incessantly,
Making it full of inner light and heat :
As when on holy ground he bared his feet
Watching the harmless flame to heaven ascend,
And talk'd with the Most High, as friend with friend.
So, courteous and unfearing he stood there,
As one to whom all places equal were,
And equal to all presences : and bore
Like a light load his threescore years and more.

Then said the King :

          ' Osarsiph, for I hear
' That thou art wise in all our lore, and dear
' To many in the land, fain would I see
' What holy power and wisdom is with thee.'

Then he : ' I am obedient to thy word,
' O King, what thing soever thou hast heard.
' The Most High, whom alone I serve and know,
' Will what He will upon His slave bestow.'

Then budding osier-twigs in rows they lay,
And strip them white, and cast the bark away.
And every priest his osier-rod throws down,
Which leaps and flashes to a serpent brown
And with a sudden hiss passes from sight.

Osarsiph also takes an osier white,
And on the polish'd floor the rod throws down,
Which leaps and flashes to a serpent brown
And with a sudden hiss passes from sight.

' The Gods are equal : equal is the fight '
The people shout.

              ' Ye foolish ones, not so :
' From Amoûn's hand all signs and wonders flow.
' The blessèd ones e'en from the bad man's eyes
' Withdraw not all the secrets of the skies ;

‘ For Typhôn guards his sons, and Horus smiles
‘ To see the wicked trapp’d in his own wiles.
‘ And other wonders, past his word and spell,
‘ The God allots to those who love him well.
‘ But first, as we would do the right by all,
‘ Upon our slave, Osarsiph, here we call
‘ In whose name, by whose power, he does this thing.’

So from his chair of splendour spoke the King
Seemingly just : but he, in sober phrase,
        .   ‘ Not unto us, not unto us, the praise,
‘ Royal Amenophis, for this or aught.
‘ The God who from far lands our fathers brought,
‘ The God Most High, working through me this sign,
‘ Has put a word in my mouth, even mine.
‘ Alone by his own will he made all things,
‘ El-Shaddai, Lord of Lords, and King of Kings.
‘ The sun and stars. the sea and the dry land
‘ Are dust within the hollow of his hand ;
‘ The nations and their Gods being nought before
‘ This only one who is for evermore.
‘ His house is not in temples made by hands,
‘ Or where the altar and the offering stands ;
‘ For earth and skies and all that is in them
‘ Are but the waving of his garment-hem.
‘ How should ye climb up to his presence thus ?
‘ We may not see him, as he sees through us.
‘ And he within my heart has put this word :
‘ The groaning of his people he has heard,

Q

' And bids thee lift the burden from their back
' Or ' . . . .

But at this a roaring, hoarse and black,
Went up throughout the hall, as when the dyke
Breaks, and the boulder-rocks and waters strike
Down the doom'd vale in thunder : and some were
Who call'd to smite him to the pavement bare,
With glittering eyes and teeth, and frantic cry,
And noise of hands, and falchions flash'd on
    high.
But, smiling 'neath his beard, he calmly stood
(God being with him) mid the riot rude,
As one who knows his time is not yet come,
A willing exile from the promised home.
Likewise the King survey'd the tumult hoarse
Calmly, nor loth to give the flood its course,
And then to silence waved, and briefly said
' Son of Paapis, he is with the dead.
' But first, for we would bring the slave to shame
' Lest, after death, the followers use his name,
' Let us entreat that Horus, through our hand,
' Shall work some sign that he cannot withstand
' Or equal or undo.'

      So silence reigns
One hour throughout the hall, and each refrains
Almost from very breath, lest Horus' ire
Should smite with arrowy storm of forkéd fire.
Now sacrifice is done, and embers red
Glow like faint rubies on each altar-head,

And smoke and incense cloud the noontide air.
When lo ! obedient to the sage's prayer
A globe of light, that none can gaze upon,
Liquid and large hangs o'er the ivory throne,
And in it work and waver sapphire wings
And eyes of hawks and fearful nameless things.
And all men veil'd their faces, and fell prone
And cried 'Amoûn is God, and he alone.'
Osarsiph also bow'd, as if to one
Seen clear in far-off heaven, beyond the sun,
Speaking with Him, who by the burning tree
Said, *Of a surely I will be with thee :*
' And if so, O if ever, now ! O God,
' Pitying thine own beneath the bitter rod
' In the dark house of bondage . . .'
                                    And he sigh'd.
---—Then in one moment darkness o'er the wide
Hall, and great Memphis, and all Egypt fell ;
Close clinging darkness, like the soot of hell.
First one sheer shriek among the crowd arose,
Then murmurs seething down to blank repose ;
As bees when brimstone fills the hive atop
Hum fierce and high, then fold their wings and drop
So sat the throng that eyeless gloom beneath,
And each held other's hands, and thought it death
But in the Syrian dwellings there was light.
        Softly they then withdrew beneath the night,
And none else stirr'd, till o'er the land afeard
The three days wept-for dawn [1] at length appear'd.

[1] See Note

Now when Amenophis saw his might defied,
He call'd the lords of Egypt to his side,
And the decree went forth How all that bow'd
Before Osarsiph's God, the leprous crowd,
Shepherds and herdsmen, East-North-East should go,
Where the great quarries lie, a land of woe,
And leave the holy soil of Egypt free
From the white plague and foul impiety.
    'Twas added also, ' Let a leaden cone
' Over each leper, fitting him, be thrown,
' And he be cast within the Eastern sea.'

So through the whole land roll'd the loud decree,
Mendés to Ipsambûl.   And though the few,
True to Osarsiph as their chieftain true,
Look'd for some aid from God, some pity shown,
The bitter day went by, and yet was none.
Then from their reedy huts and caves of mud
The royal soldiers, like the rising flood
Of Nilus round some village, chase the crowd,
Old men and youths and babes a-wailing loud,
And women's cries ; but the men mostly dumb,
Quitting hard days for harder days to come.
The red Egyptian and the Ethiop black
Mock'd that brown rabble on its painful track ;
' Ye godless slaves, be these your Gods ye bear,
' In baskets upon asses, rich and rare' ?
For sordid loads, in sooth, the exiles bore :
Broken utensils, tatter'd rags and poor

Treasures ; beneath, what gold and arms they had.
But Hope went not beside that army sad ;
Stubborn Persistance only, with keen teeth
Together clench'd, and fix'd immutable Faith.

Behind them crawl'd the lepers, white-hair'd, thin,
Starr'd with bright spots that ate below the skin,
And eyes that glared like wild things in despair,
Beneath the blazing skies outcast and bare.
Gray rolls of lead they dragg'd, each twelve a load,
And soldiers scourged them on the knee-deep road.

Along a terrace, where they pass'd the gate,
Amenophis and his lords to watch them sate
On ivory chairs, with purple canopied,
Fork'd pennons streaming o'er them, blue and
    red.
Osarsiph also, bound, was set beside.
    Then his true wife went by, who vainly tried
With yearning hands to touch his feet, and kiss,
Saying ' Is this the end, the promise this ' ?
    So she pass'd on among the common herd.
But he look'd down, and spoke no single word.
    And in likewise went by his eldest son,
The first fruits of his love, the dearest one,
Bleeding and bound, and raised a bitter cry
' I go to death : but wilt thou let me die,
' Father ' . . . then on among the common herd.
But he look'd down, and spoke no single word.

Last came there one with white unshelter'd head,
And war-scarr'd limbs, half-hid in patch and shred,
Who to the King stretch'd up his wither'd palms,
And for his utter misery ask'd an alms.
And then Osarsiph beat his breast, and wept.
    And the King marvell'd : ' Wherefore hast thou kept
' Thy grief for this one, who is none of thine ' ?
    And he : ' Because *they* were too nearly mine.
' But, seeing him, I weep the wrong I see,
' That after righteous days such end should be.
' How long, O God, how long shall it be thus ?
' O God our hope ; hast thou forgotten us ' ?

Then the King also wept at hearing him.
And Anaïs, where she lay, the maiden slim,
Crouch'd by the chair, knelt on her knees upright
And touch'd the King's knees and his raiment white,
And scarce could cry his mercy on the man,
Her mouth so fill'd with sobs as she began.
' Though he be bound for death, yet bid him go :
' Such tears, falling unwiped, will work us woe.'
So they unloosed and bade him go his way ;
And the King said ' Osarsiph, as a prey
' Thy life I give thee back, to thine own woe.'
' Yea,' answer'd he, ' but, if God wills, e'en so.'
' Fool, it is not thy God who bids thee live,
' But I, that will, to take life or to give.'
    Then said he : ' I shall see thy face no more.
' But thou, in other days, when these are o'er,

' Only one hour to see my face shalt pray.
' But He thou mockest shall mock thee that day.'
     Now from the black earth and the blazing green
Of those bank-sides the brown Nile slips between,
A little march athwart the wheaten land
The wanderers traverse to the desert strand.
Far as the blessèd waters rise and flow,
So far the emeraldine meadows go ;
At a step almost, then, from life's green domain
To the white ashes and the pebbly plain ;—
The din of the great cities and the cry
Of labourers in the millet fields and rye,
And creaking dredge-wheels and the Linus song
Making one chorus the whole valley long,—
And the black silence of that horrid plain :
 So nigh, there, life and death hold their domain.
As midsea sailors silent at the bows
Watch the small strip of yellow deck, that ploughs
The furrow of life the barren blue athwart.
   But on the people so the scene had wrought,
That here Typhón and Horus once, men said,
The Powers of Good and Evil, combated ;
And in their combat strange the poison breath
Of dark Typhón well-nigh work'd Horus' death.
For that grim Power took strength continually
From Earth below, who shot forth mountains
    high
To lend him foothold, till, with sudden clasp
Uplifted high in Horus' mighty grasp

(Whom Athor-Isis strengthen'd with new strength) ;—
O'er giant Evil Good triumph'd at length.
But the sad scene, with its dark tales of old,
Woes present, coming miseries manifold,
With such despair upon the lorn ones press'd,
E'en on those scorching sands they thought to rest ;
And there had perish'd, had not God before
Spread a green mirage, to allure them o'er :
And ghostly shafts of light, and mist between,
Like pillars winding o'er the waste were seen.
So guided, they paced on.
                              But when what gleam'd
So fair and fresh, another Nile it seem'd,
At even-fall a pool of salt they found,
And a few bitter herbs on the white ground,
They drew Osarsiph out, with curse and cry,
Like wolves in circle : ' Stone him, that he die.'
But forth his sister Miriam, where she stood
With kind hands busy for the multitude
Binding the footsore children of the crowd,
Came, and with passionate gesture cried aloud
' Not him, not him, but me ; the eldest one :
' He might have made his peace ; I urged him on.'
Then others said : ' Let both together die !
' Better to fall in Egypt, manfully,
' Than here of thirst, like beasts.'
                              Whereat their chief :
' Let be, for surely will He grant relief.'
And on the bitter pool his staff he threw,

As one who knows that, whatso'er he do,
The end has come. But when the people drew,
They drank, and were refresh'd ; for it was sweet.
And they fell down, and kiss'd Osarsiph's feet.

Yet, as men redden oft the gray-blue steel
In furnace plunged, anon in ice anneal,
To put the keenest temper on its edge,
E'en so 'tis aye the nation's privilege
Fated to great things, to be greatly tried.
And when they reach'd the allotted mountain-side
And the stern quarries, many times they said
' Better it were in Egypt, 'mong the dead.'
For there, the green fields and the blessèd Nile :
Here, the bare rocks and thorny herbage vile :
There, the slim fruitful palm, that waves on high
His happy canopies 'gainst a laughing sky ;
Here, the dwarf plant upon the stony shelf,
With barren boughs low-twisted on itself,
Like a slave crook'd with toil, and every limb
So bent, man's form is well nigh gone from him.
Thus also bent the people 'neath their toil,
In the fire burn'd, yet not consumed.
                                        Meanwhile
Those were dark years, whilst, where the sunblanch'd
        rocks
Lay crowding o'er the plain, like folded flocks,
Or in the quarries, where the limestone ledge
Went climbing up the precipice,— edge on edge

Crawling like ants, they labour'd at the stone.
Pale spaces and keen blue above them shone,
And stars went by, gazing down pitiless
Upon their iron toil, and long duresse,
Rounding the back, and parching up each limb.
No cheering green ; no water-voice ; but grim
And silent the dead desert, round its prey.

But whilst in the red furnace thus they lay,—
The drowsihood of Egypt, the soul's rust,
The life according to the flesh, and lust,
Soft selfishness of city luxuries,
And hardening want, that has no hope to rise ;
The baser nature in the slave begot,
Who, treated beast-like, beast-like learns to rot ;—
The boastings of vain science, that could give
Blessings to life, whilst she untaught to live ;
The boastings of vain priesthoods, who deny
All ways to God, but what themselves supply,
The sensual impulse of the gorgeous rite,
The myriad Gods, that hid the One from sight :
    All this, the fire of Heaven burn'd out from them ;
And a new heart within the people came,
Raising to higher things than yet they dream'd.

God also was more near them than He seem'd
In multitudinous Egypt, where the sighs
And glare and steam of life o'er-hazed the skies.

—For though man gains from man, yet something then
Of higher nature slips beyond his ken,
Nor does the heart within the heart speak plain,
Till to the lonely land he turns again,
In valleys, where the still small voices brood,
And hints of Heaven that flash through solitude :—
There in blue fire the silver summits rest,
Scored with a thousand secrets on their breast :
There, snow and sapphire mingled as they go,
Wild murmuring messages down the torrents flow :—
—O hall of audience for high converse fit !
Where the All speaks with man, and he with It ;
And drinks the free fresh life of mountain peace,
Learning himself in the waste wilderness.

BOOK III

MEANTIME the King, as one secure from ill,
His foes withdrawn, work'd out his utmost will,
And the long vale of Nile, from side to side,
From North to South-ward, swept and purified,
Bringing the land back to her earlier ways.
  Now, as gray herons, whom men and dogs upraise
From their still mere, and scatter through the copse,
When those they fear are gone, from the tree-tops
(Their leader calling them with one shrill cry)
Come down and o'er the mere in ecstasy
One moment skim, with outstretch'd neck and bent ;
Then settle in their haunts down, well content,
Lords of the place, to dig and dive for food,
  So back on Egypt came the multitude
Of her strange-headed Gods, and crowd the soil

Then in the polish'd temples, by long toil
Cameo'd with acts of kings, and holy names,
From low-built altars sparkled the white flames,
Incense, and fat of sheep, and phoenix-root.
And Buto's oracle, long choked and mute,
Regain'd her voice, for counsel or to warn,
And Memnon's image sang once more at morn.

Likewise the Linus-burden *Fair, O fair*,
Each reaping-band alternate taking share,
Across the Nile, above the harvest boats,
In melancholy cadence answering floats :
And Isis on the husbandmen pours down
Her yearly blessings in the cornsheaves brown.
So to its earlier ways the land return'd,

But the King's heart, which first within him burn'd,
Raising the faith up, and from their abodes
Chasing the enemy of the blessèd Gods,
Grew cold, he knew not why ; and all his toil
Came back upon him with a dull recoil,
As when in dreamland men uproll a stone
Which ever to their hand returns anon
Making their labour piteous : and the thirst
To see the God, was hot in him as erst :
So far as light 'twas, to the light was true,
Yet to his heart's desire no nearer drew.
So sate he crown'd with care, and sick at ease.

'All has been done, that should Osiris please ;
'His foes driven out ; the whole land once more
    his :
'The God is debtor to Amenophis.
'Should he not pay, shall I pay sacrifice ?
'Alas ! but I can aid me thus nowise.
'For, seen or unseen, satisfied or irate,
'The Gods are there, and masters of our fate.

' Yet if I saw him once, then might I know
' Whether our prayers and deeds reach him, or no.
' I must be sure here, or in doubt of all.
' For the great vision I, the Pharaoh, call !
' However named, however form'd, appear :
' The King of Kings can look on thee, and bear.'
Thus thinking, he survey'd the pictured wall,
And watch'd the flushing sunbeam softly crawl
O'er Rhampsinitus, red and huge of limb,
Dicing with Isis in Amenthes dim.

   Then with quick steps a Nubian, crisp-hair'd, small,
White-girded, broke the silence of the hall :
Holding above his head a letter seal'd,
And said ' This for the King of Kings,' and kneel'd.
But when Amenophis took it, he was gone.
And the King, wondering, read the scroll anon.

   The dead son of Paapis to the King.
' From dark Amenthes this last word I bring :
' Because thou hast, among the leprous throng,
' Driven hence a holy priest, doing him wrong,
' Who now in the great quarry, a brown speck
' Beneath the ledgy rocks, and o'er his neck
' A halter hung, wearied and shrunk in limb,
' Melts his life down, a soldier scourging him,
' Though he has trodden where the angels trod,
' Holding free converse with the most high God,
' And seeing that, which thou shalt never see,—
' I then, son of Paapis, say to thee

' Repent thee of this thing, and set him free.
' For I who counsell'd thee to do this wrong
' Am call'd away from life, in mid-age strong,
' From pleasures, and all sweet things on the earth.
' From wisdom, and from wisdom's inner mirth
' When a man thinks of all he knows,--but then
' Dies down among the herd of common men,
' And is like me, a shade, and man no more.'

Then the King shouted, and his raiment tore,
Like one who suddenly to madness goes
From reason calm, nor his own purpose knows,
Nor what he was, remembers ; but despair
Folds round him as a robe, closer than air ;
Sitting like stone : and should the world go by,
The show of it had not reach'd his absent eye.

Only a memory murmur'd in his brain
Restless and saying low *The toil is vain :*
That also, *Thou to see my face shall pray,*
But he thou mockest shall mock thee that day.

Then far off, faint, like insect voices fine
Heard and not heard, when midday sunbeams shine
On meadows, where the golden grasses rear
Their spiked array above the listener's ear,
High notes, in intermittent strain, stole through
Where the King sate, and mingled with his woe :
But he just raised his hand, as though to chase
Some clear-wing'd gauzy minstrel from his face.

Next, four-string'd lyres, as near the music draws,
With webs of rich embroidery fill'd each pause,
And mellow chords beat undulating low
Like throbs from happy hearts that overflow
With too much happiness.

                Anon they stand
Before the throne, the Lydian chorus-band :
And now, as one who thanks the Gods,[1] restored
To life from sickness, a full strain they pour'd,
Sweetness unearthly, solemn blissfulness :—
Now, as if new force came within them, press
Hurried, and bounding high : then, gliding, toy
With the low notes, and sighs of utter joy.
Last, a gay march like wreathèd pearls flung round.
Then one sang out, in words of Lydian sound :

' Return, Adonis, for the Hours are near :
' Return, Cythérè : thy beloved is here.
' The long months' tomb hath hid each dainty limb ;
' O bitter frost-months, parting her and him !
' Seal'd in the barren cave he may forget,
' But Cypris Queen sighs and remembers yet,—
' The hyacinth beds, that from the pinewood dip,
' The little Loves that flew from lip to lip
' Like birds from bough to bough, and all that bliss :—
' O Cypris dear ! and yet to end in this !
' —Diónè's child, lament him now no more ;
' The Hours Adonis to thine arms restore.

                [1] See Note

' Lo here for thee and here for him we spread
' The ivory couch, and smooth the purple bed :
' O young Adonis, crown for us the year !
' Sick with delay, let thy fair face appear ;
' Here with the violet-crown'd take up thy rest ;
' Blest in thy coming, in thy going blest.'

So Anaïs fair sang, and before the throne
Crouch'd and her eyes hid, when the rest were
    gone.
  But from his heart meanwhile despair had fled,
By the soft touch of music banishéd,
And the consoling passion of that strain :
And calmer blood came back into his brain,
And hopes and thoughts more fitting man's estate.
  Then on a low stool at his feet she sate,
Drawing the gauze over her breast, and laid
Her head into his hands, and smiled, and said,

' O Lord and King, if I may speak thee aught
' Of counsel, (thou being wise, and Anaïs nought),
. But 'tis not so as thou this thing hast done
' That in my country men the God have won,
' As, chasing them who other altars prize,
' Or taking heaven by storm with instant cries.
' For in their quiet seats They sit and smile.
' And though 'tis said their forms were seen erewhile
' By mortal men, as those round Ilios slain,
' Aiding the Heroes in their toil and pain,

R

' Yet at their own good will from heaven they shot,
' Like lightning flashes keen, and then were not.
' Likewise as though by chance, at moments when
' None reck'd : as he of the Arcadian glen,
' Laphanés, Euphorion's son, the shining Two
' Housed in Azania : or where, neath the snow
' Of Bermion, mid the gardens of the King,
' The sixty-petall'd roses burn in spring,
' And men came by and caught Silenus there
' Sleep-flush'd and rose-drunk in the lavish air.
   ' But far from me, my Lord, may such things
     lie !
' Lest I should see the blesséd ones, and die :—
' But I would live ; what pleasure is in death ?
' For we have but a cubit's span of breath,
' The gnat's one-day life ; and, e'en thus, the sun
' Oft hides his face, ere our brief line be run.
' Let me be so, or let me cease to be.—
' O young Adonis, thus I envy thee,
' Having no frozen age, but in thy bloom
' Closed in the chambers of the restful tomb !

Then he : ' O little heedful of thy doom !
' As though indeed this one fair hour of love
' Were all the circle, neath us, and above !
' Whilst, deep in central space, Osiris sits
' Judging the soul, as from the corpse it flits,
' Whether it willeth not, or if it will.
' And Horus holds the scale of Good and Ill,

' And he I name not, standing with his rod,
' Measures the dreadful balance for the God.
' Seek not the Babylonian star-lore vain,
' But simply bear whate'er the Powers ordain.
' For so it must be, Anaïs, even so ;
' Whether we will it, Anaïs mine, or no.
' And these things often in thy soul should'st view,
' Lest, too late waking, thou shalt find them true.
' Remember'st not the words thy kinsman sung,
' The young Aeolian minstrel to the young ?-
" —O thou too confident in the strength of youth,
" All too young yet to dread the day of truth ;
" When the sad years are white upon thy head,
" And that dark plumage of thy shoulders shed,
" And the soft blush-rose blanch'd from out the cheek,
" And from thy eloquent mirror-glass shall speak
" Another Anaïs, then, *Alas*, wilt say,
" *Why, what I think now, thought I not that day?*
" *Or why, when wisdom comes, in wisdom's train*
" *Do not the untarnish'd roses bloom again?*"

Then Anaïs soft : ' So be it, an it must !
' We are their playthings ; they are strong and just.
' And I have heard how Peleus and his son,
' Cadmus, and Herakles, and many a one
' Like them, as Gods among the Gods are set :
' Where all our night long their sun shineth yet,
' And red-rose meadows round their city fold,
' And waveless waters starr'd with flowers of gold.

' Likewise they toil not now by sea or shore,
' With the just Gods living for evermore,
' Life without tears,
                    But I would rather be
' With him that lies by Megara-on-sea,
' Diokles, who erewhile from Athens came,
' He who loved children, and was loved of them :
'--Ever around his tomb, when Spring is nigh,
' The village-youths with rival kisses vie ;
' And he who sweetest lip on lip hath press'd,
' Goes violet-crown'd, and is proclaim'd the Best.

' So would I lie, and list the whispers sweet,
' And rosy shufflings of unsandall'd feet.

'—Be these things as they may !   But O my lord
' Wilt thou not hearken to the wise man's word,
' Loosing the lepers from their misery ?
' For to the God should they be left, whom he
' Hath smitten with a heavy hand, and woe.
' Have pity on them : Let the people go.'

So Anaïs pleaded, with a woman's heart
Right to the right, and to the better part
Strove to win o'er the King.
                           But whether pride
Wrought in him for his purposes defied,
Or wrath of mere despair, some say his heart
Was harden'd, and refused the better part,
Hurling his chariots on, and seaward chased
Those whom, at Heaven's command, the waves
    embraced

As friends, and yielded passage ; but the host
Of Egypt and her King were sunk and lost.
For as a mountain torrent to the sea
So rush'd all Egypt's might confusedly,
And the sea claim'd his own.

                But when the morn
Came, pure and peaceful from the tempest born,
Over a plain of smiles the sunbeams glide,
And the white whispers of the rippling tide.

– But God hath also gentler ways to deal
With his own creature, and with him can feel,
Pitying his pride of heart, not smiting him.
Nor is He less within the twilight dim
Of seeking souls, than in the soul upright
That sees him face to face, and walks in light ;
Knowing all knowledge nothing before His.

Thus also fared it with Amenophis.
For other stories tell, how the King's heart
Was changed and soften'd to the better part
By Anaïs and her sweet womanliness.
And how he loosed the people from duresse,
Giving them gifts, that they should take their way
East, where the dwellings of their kinsfolk lay,
And serve the God of all, so as they chose.

Then the great King and his land had repose
A many years, and all things rich and good :
For Nilus bless'd them with his living flood,

And kine, and wine, and golden granaries.
And from the leprous taint they had release,
Cleansing the land : nor did the Lybian foe,
Nor he from far Assyria, work them woe
Wasting as locusts : nor the pirate-bands
Of Crete or Sidon, dropping on the sands,
Harry the palm-roof'd cabin-huts, or those
In cities, where the seven-branch'd Nile outflows.
But when the time was now fulfill'd, that he
Should go, where man at length the God may see.
Then Anaïs, being younger, was afraid
Lest she alone should linger, life-delay'd.
So, going to the shrine, the God besought,
That if her faithfulness had merit aught,
He would vouchsafe them what for man was best.

Thus having pray'd, she took the maiden vest
Wherein she cross'd the seas, and crown'd her head.
Likewise the King came robed and garlanded ;
And sacrifice was held, and feasting high.
Then, where close-veil'd from touch of human eye
The image of great Isis darkly gleams,
Within the furthest shrine, a place of dreams,
Silent, before the smouldering altar-brand,
With the last kisses, and the hand on hand,
They fell on sleep together where they lay ;
Awaking to the long, long, better Day.

NOTES

AND

INDEX OF FIRST LINES

NOTES

PAGE 4 *As when* . . . In the old Welsh tale, the *Mabinogi* of Bronwen, the Birds of Rhiannon (perhaps a Lake-nymph, and mother to Pryderi), sang the dead to life and the living to sleep. Brân Fendigaid (the Blessed) plays a great and mysterious part in these early legends : he was son to Llyr Llediaith, King of Britain ; and one tradition makes him bring Christianity into the island. Brân was slain in Ireland, and his sister Bronwen (white-bosomed), dying of grief, was buried by the Alaw in Anglesey : where, in accordance with the legend, her bones, placed in a foursquare stone grave, were found at a spot called Vnys Bronwen in 1813. Brân's head, carried to the White Mount (the Tower) of London, whilst undisturbed, guarded the Island from invasion. (Lady C. Guest, the *Mabinogion*, and Rhys, *Arthurian Legend*.)

―――― *Ardudwy* . . . One of the six ancient districts of Merioneth.

PAGE 5 *That great seer* . . . Homer : *cf.*

> —μάλα πολλὰ μεταξύ,
> οὔρεά τε σκιόεντα θάλασσά τε ἠχήεσσα.
> —*Iliad* I, 156-7.

PAGE 79 *The three stars*, which first appeared, were taken as the signal whence to reckon evening by the Jews in Our Saviour's time. (Edersheim, *Messiah*.)

PAGE 122 *Desideratissimae :*

> —δάκρυα παρέξω · ταῦτα γὰρ δυναίμεθ' ἄν.
> —*Iph. in Aul.* 1115.

PAGE 131 *Peace* . . . A splendid fragment, from a Paean by the lyrical poet Bacchylides,

> Τίκτει δέ τε θνατοῖσιν Εἰράνα . . .

is here paraphrased.

PAGE 136 *By the Furies won* . . . See the terrible ὕμνος ἐξ Ἐρινύων in the *Eumenides* of Aeschylus.

PAGE 150 *That pure master-piece* . . . The colossal statue of San Carlo stands upon a hill close to Arona on the Lago Maggiore. Within the Church of S. Maria degli Angeli is the lovely picture of the Nativity, by Gaudenzio Ferrari, here alluded to.

PAGE 152 *The Lament of Argathelia.* For the early descent of the House of Argyll reference has been here made to the great historical works of Skene and Joseph Robertson.

PAGE 153 *Between beauty and goodness: . . . cf.* Dante:
— tra bella e buona
Non so che fosse più—

PAGE 157 Severn, by a few pictures of merit and interest : Wells, by his early poem, *Joseph and his Brethren;*—seemed to promise work worthy the friends of Keats.

PAGE 164 *A Pause before Battle.* Horatia, reputed daughter by Lord Nelson of Lady Hamilton, born 1799, spent her infancy and childhood at Merton. A letter from Nelson to her mother says, " I beg, as my dear little Horatia is to be at Merton, that a strong netting, about three feet high, may be placed round the Nile [a streamlet in the garden, so named by Lady Hamilton], that the little thing may not tumble in." Horatia married the Rev. P. Ward, and died on March 6, 1881. (*Times,* March 10, 1881.)

PAGE 183 *Chloris* . . . in the Greek mythology, figures the fresh golden green of Spring.

PAGE 197 *The Mount that wears the cap* . . . Mons Pil[e]atus: So named from its frequent cloud-covering.

PAGE 227 *Cf.* Dante's phrase

—la molt' anni lagrimata pace.

PAGE 240 *As one who thanks the Gods* . . . To lovers of music this passage may faintly recall the marvellous Quartet in A minor (Op. 132),—Beethoven's hymn upon recovery from severe illness. In the central portion of this Poem without words, the solemn *Canzone Lidico* of thanksgiving is soon followed by the brilliant outburst, marked *Sentendosi nuova forza.*

INDEX OF FIRST LINES

www.ingramcontent.com/pod-product-compliance
Lightning Source LLC
Chambersburg PA
CBHW031347020726
47499CB00005B/1433